Christmas at the Cottage

an Oyster Bay novel

Olivia Miles

~ Rosewood Press ~

Also by Olivia Miles

The Oyster Bay Series
Feels Like Home
Along Came You
Maybe This Time
This Thing Called Love
Those Summer Nights

The Misty Point Series
One Week to the Wedding
The Winter Wedding Plan

Sweeter in the City Series
Sweeter in the Summer
Sweeter Than Sunshine
No Sweeter Love
One Sweet Christmas

The Briar Creek Series
Mistletoe on Main Street
A Match Made on Main Street
Hope Springs on Main Street
Love Blooms on Main Street
Christmas Comes to Main Street

Harlequin Special Edition
'Twas the Week Before Christmas
Recipe for Romance

This is a work of fiction. Names, characters, businesses, places, events and incidents are either the products of the author's imagination or used in a fictitious manner. Any resemblance to actual persons, living or dead, or actual events is purely coincidental.

ISBN 978-0-9995284-5-7
CHRISTMAS AT THE COTTAGE

First Edition: November 2018

Christmas at the Cottage

an Oyster Bay novel

Chapter One

Kelly Myers was having a pinch-me moment. She was here. In Oyster Bay. She'd actually done it. Packed up her bags and rented a cottage, and not just any cottage, mind you…a cottage with a name. White Pine Cottage. How cute was that? It was seriously so perfect, she almost couldn't believe it was real.

But it was real. All of it. From the evergreen wreaths hanging from lampposts by fat, red, velvety ribbons to the twinkle lights framing each storefront window to the mounds of snow that were piled high along the sidewalks. And so much snow! So much snow, in fact, that it appeared to be not falling from the sky, per se, but rather flying horizontally, causing people at the crosswalk to walk with their heads down, their bodies bent at the waist, in a somewhat awkward attempt to push through the wind.

Okay, so that was a little troubling. She had her knitwear: hats, cowls, scarves, mittens. She had her wool peacoat, which had been more than warm enough for the last two San Francisco winters, and which she thought would suffice in Maine, with a warm turtleneck sweater layered underneath for insurance. But now she saw that the women clutching shopping bags were wearing down coats that went past their knees. And boots that were thick and functional, not stylish like the saddle brown leather ones Kelly was wearing.

Well, perhaps today was a one-off. Perhaps tomorrow would be better. It would be, she was sure, because how could every aspect of this experience not be absolutely wonderful? She was going to spend her very first Christmas with both of her sisters. Together they would do all the things that they hadn't been able to do together when they were younger, things she personally had never done during the holidays. She had an entire list to cover, right down to sledding on Shell Hill—something that Hannah had talked about every winter when she was living in California, reminiscing about all the fun stuff she used to do with her sister, until she caught herself and covered her mouth, her eyes guilty as she said, "Sorry, Kel. I meant, my other sister."

What she'd meant was her real sister. Her full sister, Evie. The sister she'd grown up with, in their dad's house in this cozy, idyllic town, not the sister she didn't meet until she was eighteen years old. It was a slip, but one that happened often over the years, always leaving Kelly to wonder what that made her. A distant relative? Kelly always felt the sting but brushed it off quickly. It was a small price to pay to hear more about Evie, who still remained a mystery, even if they did email and text and chat on the phone now.

But soon that would all change. Soon, tomorrow in fact, she would meet Evie in person. And then Hannah could no longer refer to Evie as her sister. No, now Hannah would have to refer to Evie as *their* sister.

Kelly nearly squealed with excitement, but she wasn't sure how the cab driver would feel about this, so she pressed her lips together firmly and stared out the window. They were almost out of town now, the quaint restaurants and shops were turning to picket fences and white wooden houses with Christmas trees visible through their front windows. Kelly turned and craned her neck back at the town, wishing she had taken a better look at the office of the *Oyster Bay Gazette* as they passed it, imagining both her sisters inside, hard at work. She had considered surprising them, considering they weren't expecting her flight to get in until after ten tonight, but she'd been so eager, she'd gotten to the airport before the crack of dawn and snagged a standby ticket.

But no, she thought, turning in her seat again, tomorrow was the best time to meet Evie, as planned. Showing up unannounced might be awkward, and besides, Kelly wasn't so sure she was ready just yet either.

Tonight she would settle into the cottage, hang some holiday decorations she'd packed in her suitcase, and get a good night's rest for the big weekend.

She sat up straighter as the driver turned onto a winding road, or rather, slid onto it, nearly colliding with the trunk of a massive pine that prompted him to curse under his breath.

He put the gear in park and turned over the seat back to look at her. "That's as far as I go."

"What?" She blinked, torn from the beauty of her surroundings much too suddenly. Where she was from, she was used to door to door service. She looked out the window, at the snow, bewildered. "But where's the cottage?"

"Follow the drive. Bear to the right. You'll reach it."

"But—" Kelly frowned at this and studied her options. The road seemed to fork, and the path to the right did not look promising. "But it's not plowed."

"Exactly. Now this is as far as I go." He held out his hand, and with a sigh, Kelly eyed the meter and then thrust the cash at him.

"Nice tip," he said, sounding surprised. "For that, I'll even help you with your bags."

Oh! Now this wasn't so bad, especially since she hadn't exactly packed light. Here she'd pegged him for a Scrooge, when he really might have some holiday spirit in him after all. She was here for a three-week stay, through to the New Year, and winter clothes sure were bulky. She opened the door and nearly closed it again when a gust of downright arctic air hit her full force, but no, no, this was part of the experience! The cold, very cold, painfully cold in fact, yet still delightful experience.

This is what she had wanted. Dreamed of, even. Ever since she was *fourteen* years old and Hannah described how she and Evie used to have themes for their snowmen. She wanted to build a snowman. And she wanted it to have a theme. And it didn't matter that she was now twenty-five. Better late than never.

She was just starting to feel better when the cab driver slammed the trunk and said, "Have a nice visit."

Kelly opened her mouth to protest, but it was too late. He was in his car. His warm, toasty car, and she was…knee deep in snow with four rolling suitcases and a duffel bag stacked against a tree. Bah-humbug, indeed!

The wind was howling and the snow was so heavy she could barely see through it. She could ask the man to bring her back to town, wait it out, have a coffee and then try again in an hour or so. Only something told her it might not be an hour before this let up. And besides, the cottage couldn't be too far if he was willing to drop her off here. She'd grab half the bags now and the other upon her return.

With a lift of her chin, she started to walk, sliding the two suitcases behind her, cursing at herself for lugging holiday decorations across the country when the cottage was probably already decorated for the season anyway, hoping that the remaining luggage wouldn't get stolen in her absence. Just to be sure, she turned and checked a few times to make sure they were there. On the third try, when she stopped to catch her breath, her eyes shot open when she saw a red pickup truck parked where the cab had been and a man climbing out of the driver seat, frowning at the pile of her belongings.

"Wait!" she cried, dropping the handles of the suitcases and letting them fall to the snow. She did a mental calculation of potential breakables...a few ornaments, her favorite tree topper-- Oh, she'd worry about that later. "Those are mine!"

She was slipping, and the snow made running harder than sand did. The man seemed to pause—maybe he had realized he'd been caught, a-ha!—and stood watching her. A strange glint in his eye was obvious when she approached, panting and sweating and so out of breath she was actually afraid that she might throw up right then and there at the base of his weather-appropriate boots.

There was a time when she used to hit the gym every day. But then Brian dumped her for her friend Shannon, and then Brian and Shannon got the gym and she got...a fresh start, she told herself firmly. Winter. Christmas. Snow. Sisters! All good things. No thinking about men allowed. Especially the kind that were prone to break your heart.

"Those are mine," she said, so out of breath that no sound really came out. She reached down and grabbed the handles of her suitcases and pulled them toward her, awkwardly.

The man looked at her quizzically, and she realized with a flicker of embarrassment that he was reasonably young. Maybe even…handsome, some might say. Not her, though. Nope! She'd sworn off men. Still, he wasn't exactly the vicious thief she had made him out to be. If anything, he seemed downright confused instead of malicious.

"Where are you going?" he asked, his eyes appraising her as he leaned back on his heels.

His eyes were blue, almost turquoise, and so steady that she couldn't help but squirm. Her heart rate still hadn't quite returned to normal and she was breathing deeply, taking in large gulps of the freezing air that made her lungs burn. "To the White Pine Cottage," she said a little smugly, wondering if she should be giving out this information to a stranger. Still, she revealed this detail with pride, seeing as it was her first real adult trip, and her first real attempt to spend time with her family here in this town. All her life, she'd been kept away, but now, now she was able to finally claim a stake and embrace what was rightfully hers. The man's expression seemed to flicker for a moment, as if he were surprised by this information. "Why do you ask?"

"Well, I was going to offer to give you a lift," he said, a slight curl forming at the corners of his mouth. "Seeing as…"

"I'm struggling?"

"I was going to say, seeing as the driveway hasn't been

plowed," he said. "But now that you mention it…" He grinned a little. Some might say mockingly.

Her temper flared and she gripped the handles of the suitcases a little tighter. "I'm just fine, thank you very much."

He arched an eyebrow, and okay, yes, she realized that he was handsome by definition. Appeal, though, was something altogether different. He was smug and cocky, and he was having fun at her expense. And this trip was supposed to be special, damn it. It wasn't supposed to be full of snow and wet feet and, oh, God, she was shaking now. She wondered if her lips were blue.

"If you insist," he said, reaching for the handle of his truck.

She eyed it, carefully, wondering if he was calling her bluff. The truck was warm. She could feel the heat from the open door, hear the purr of the radio that cut through the silent, brittle air. Talk radio. He closed the door and still she waited, half expecting him to roll down a window and say he insisted, that after all, it was practically a blizzard out here.

But instead he gave a funny grin that she could only assume was at her expense and then, off he went, leaving her standing at the base of the driveway to her magical Christmas cottage, with half of her rolling luggage and two feet of snow and shoes that were certainly not waterproof, even though they were, technically speaking, boots. They were what her friend Lindsay would call fashion boots. Leather, knee-high, looked adorable with jeans tucked in and a long sweater…

Well.

Seeing no other choice, she dragged the two suitcases to where her others sat, now half-buried in snow but visible enough. She searched through the trees, looking for a hint of a cozy cottage, like the one advertised in the online version of the *Oyster Bay Gazette*, which she now read religiously, seeing as her sister Evie still had a daily advice column and Hannah took all the photos, even though come the first of the year, Evie's column was going to be syndicated, spread out across the country. Meanwhile, Kelly had been unemployed since September.

But no use to dwell on that now! After all, if she had a job, could she take three weeks off to spend here, in this wonderful, quaint, New England town? Would she be hauling her luggage behind her, frozen to the bone, the promise of the wood-burning fireplace and the "country kitchen" the only thing keeping her from sitting down on the duffel bag and bursting into tears?

She had January to buckle down. After all, no one hired during the holidays. Everyone knew that.

She was actually starting to sweat now, which she hadn't thought possible, but her skin was still cold, and she starting to ponder the symptoms of frostbite. She worked out a system, so she wouldn't have to trek all the way back to the road when she finally reached her cozy home away from home. She dragged two suitcases ten feet, parked them, then went back, looped the duffel over her neck, and grabbed the remaining two suitcases, all the way cursing the man from the red truck.

She did this about fifteen times when finally, there, behind a cluster of pine trees, a house came into view.

A tiny house. A really, really tiny house, actually. One window sat on either side of the front door, and frost had collected on the glass. For some reason she'd imagined it would be a sunny yellow, or a perky blue, but instead it was white, and in desperate need of a fresh coat of paint. Black shutters framed the windows, and one was off its hinge. She'd expected a cheerful wreath on the door, a welcome mat even, and the fire to already be burning, smoke pouring from the chimney, waiting for her arrival. Instead the cottage looked, well, abandoned…

For a moment Kelly wondered if she had made a mistake. Given the wrong address to the driver. She remembered the funny look on the man's face when she told him all too happily that she was staying at the White Pine Cottage.

This couldn't be it. Except…There. Tacked to the side of the house, just above the mailbox, was the faded sign: White Pine Cottage.

This was it. No denying it now. Who cared if it needed some fresh paint? The howling wind probably knocked that shutter loose just this morning!

She was here. In Oyster Bay. And everything was going to be perfect.

*

They hadn't expected her so early, Kelly reasoned. That had to be it. She wasn't really due for another seven hours, and they hadn't had time to set up the accommodations. She should have called, explained her early arrival, but when her name had been called for the early flight, she'd been too busy managing her four suitcases over to the check-in desk to think about other details.

It took her all of five minutes to realize that there was no heat in the cottage. And that the wood-burning fireplace that had been advertised didn't come with a pile of wood as she'd imagined. And that the sweat that had accumulated under her coat from hauling her luggage was now turning clammy and cold and she was shivering so hard that her teeth were starting to rattle.

She eyed her bags that were resting on the mat near the front door, the snow that had collected on them was not even melting into a puddle.

Surely the heat would kick on any minute. She'd just take a nice, hot shower while she waited.

Except, she soon realized, there was no hot water. In fact, the water that came from the kitchen tap, when she went to make tea, was orange. She quickly turned it off and decided to explore the rest of the house. There was the kitchen, which was about as old as the outside of the house, with white cabinets, some loose at the hinges, a small wooden table near a back door. The living space was small but cozy, with a small television, sofa and armchair, and a lovely bay window that looked out onto the snow-covered forest. Kelly lost herself in it for a moment, forgetting for a glorious and fleeting bit of time that she was very, very cold.

She flicked on a light as she walked down a short hallway, happy to see that the electricity at least worked. A bathroom and two small bedrooms, one containing a desk and chair, the other a bed with a white quilt and cheerful yellow paint on the walls. And that was it. The entire cottage, so small she could walk through it under a minute, yet a bit bigger than her apartment back in San Francisco, nonetheless.

She opened a closet, finding it empty, and realized with a start that there weren't any towels, and that, even though she'd brought four suitcases and a duffel bag from San Francisco, she hadn't thought to bring anything practical.

She'd just have to take a walk into town. The idea brightened her for one, fleeting second until she remembered how miserable that walk to the cottage had been. Still, if there were no towels, then there was probably no…

She flung open some kitchen cabinets, and then the fridge. As feared. No food. Not even a teabag or some instant coffee.

She walked back to the bedroom, which was the warmest room in the cottage, probably because it had only one window, and sat down on the bed while she dialed her sister Hannah's number. She'd ask to spend the night, just until the heating was fixed. She couldn't exactly ask Evie because they hadn't technically met yet and Evie still lived with her dad, whom Loraine, their mother, had left for Kelly's dad, and that was all just too weird for her comfort level.

Hannah answered on the third ring, sounding distracted.

"Hannah?" Kelly pulled the phone from her ear and stared at the screen. Her reception was weak. Of course it was. She was in the middle of the woods on a remote driveway that wasn't even paved.

"Kelly? Where are you? On the plane?"

"I'm here!" Here! In Oyster Bay. The flutter in her chest returned when she realized that she had done it, that this morning she had woken up in San Francisco and that tomorrow she would wake up here, a place she had only dreamed of for so many years.

A place she'd never been a part of, until now.

"You're here!" Hannah let out a squeal and Kelly did too, just for the hell of it.

"I got an earlier flight! Want to get together tonight?" It would be dark soon, Kelly judged, noticing the way the light had grown lower since the cab had dropped her off. Just how long had it taken her to trek her bags up to this house?

"I'd love to," Hannah said, and the regret in her tone nearly matched the heaviness in Kelly's chest, but not totally. Of course. They'd made plans for tomorrow and Kelly had counted on that. She'd assumed that tonight she would be jet lagged and tired and eager to rest. But now the thought of waiting another eighteen hours to see Hannah—and meet Evie!—seemed like eighteen years. And it was cold. Very, very cold. "But tonight Lucy has a school holiday pageant. I came home early to get her ready for it."

"I can come!" Kelly had heard all about Lucy, the sweet little girl who was Hannah's boyfriend Dan's daughter. She knew all the backstory, how Dan didn't want to come out to California for college all those years ago, and how they'd sort of broken up, and how he'd spent the night with another girl, and she'd gotten pregnant, and that when Dan found out, he'd ended things for good with Hannah, even though they'd reunited. It was quite a titillating story to hear as a teenager. Kelly had never tired of it, even though Hannah did tend to go on about Dan quite a bit and how he'd broken her heart. But now Dan and Hannah were happily reunited. Her happy ending had been found in a way that was almost enough to turn Kelly into a romantic again, but not quite.

"I wish you could, but it's a sold-out show. Parents are suckers for seeing their kid in a cute costume, I tell you."

"Oh. It's okay, I understand!" Of course she understood. It wasn't personal. It was just reality. Hannah had an entire life here, she always had.

"But we'll get together tomorrow. Angie's Café at ten?

I can't wait for you to meet Evie—" Suddenly Hannah paused. "What's that sound?"

My teeth, Kelly wanted to reply. Instead, she clenched her jaw and managed to say, "Sorry, I was rattling my keys."

"Well, the hotel is lovely. It's too bad you weren't able to get in at the Harper House Inn, but Bridget is booked up for the next three months, if you can believe it."

Kelly chewed her lip, wondering when she should admit that she had not taken her older sister's recommendation and booked a room at the ridiculously expensive yet perfectly lovely Oyster Bay Hotel with gorgeous guest suites that their website boasted had ocean views and room service from a five-star restaurant. The Harper House Inn, run by Hannah's cousin, she could have swung. But she was hardly in the mood to explain her lack of employment to her sister just now. After all, Hannah had somewhere to be, and Kelly...Well, Kelly did not have anywhere to be. No job. No security. Nothing to return to in California after this holiday.

Her stomach began to hurt.

Hannah muttered something, responding to a voice in the background, and came back, her voice clearer. "Sorry, Kel. They're waiting for me, and Lucy is worried we'll be late if I don't start braiding her hair soon. See you tomorrow?"

Tomorrow. Meaning no warm bed. No hot shower. No food. Until tomorrow.

Kelly ended the call and flopped backward on the bed. It creaked and then dropped half an inch under her weight.

And that was the breaking point, literally. So much for a magical country Christmas.

Chapter Two

Kelly opened her suitcase with trembling hands and pulled out every scarf she had ever knitted, which was a lot, actually, considering that knitting was pretty much all she'd done for the past three months. It kept her from fretting about her lack of job prospects, and it kept her mind from trailing to Brian, and how he'd dropped her for Shannon, who was a low talker and planned corny date nights like wine and cheese parties in front of a chick flick.

She wrapped each scarf around her neck until she could barely move, and then pulled on a hat for good measure. It had been ten minutes since she'd called the number for the caretaker provided with her reservation, listed at the bottom of the email confirming her cozy country cottage rental.

Now she looked out the window with growing impatience, whimpered a little, and then flicked on the ancient-looking radio on the counter, turning the knob until she found a station with Christmas carols, and went to work setting up the decorations she'd packed in not one, but two suitcases.

Three knitted stockings, one for her, Evie, and Hannah. She hadn't thought to bring hooks, so she set them to the side, to hang later, when she had a tree they could all decorate. For now, she draped some tinsel from the mantle and framed the window seat in the living room with twinkling lights, and when she stepped back to admire their glow, she almost forgot that she was wrapped up like a snowman and that she was still shaking like a leaf, too.

There was a knock on the door just as she was adding a second string of lights to the mantle. "About time," she muttered and walked the short distance to the front door. She flung it open, expecting to see a little old man wearing a lumberjack shirt or work overalls or utility gloves, but instead, she was face to face with the man with the red truck. The man who had left her with four suitcases and a duffel bag in the middle of a snowstorm.

"It's you," she said, narrowing her eyes.

His expression gave nothing away, but for a moment, Kelly was distracted by the blueness of those eyes, deep set under a furrowed brow.

"I received your email," he said matter of factly, stepping into the cottage. "Something to do with the heat?"

"Or lack thereof." She moved back, letting him pass. He was tall, taller than her father, taller than Brian, and his presence filled the space, making the cottage feel even smaller, but considerably less empty.

His eyebrows shot up when his gaze lingered on the lights hanging from the mantle, but

he set his toolbox down on the kitchen counter without a word. Clearly he wasn't man for many words.

"Think you can get it fixed?"

His eyes gleamed with amusement as they roamed over her, and self-consciously, Kelly fingered the scarf (make that several scarves) at her neck. She suddenly wished she hadn't put on the variegated yarn hat with the oversized pom-pom. She'd planned to gift that one, probably to Lucy. Children were forgiving.

This man, however, was clearly not.

He didn't answer her question but instead disappeared through a door that she hadn't even noticed at the end of the kitchen. She hesitated for a moment, wondering if she should follow him, but instead stayed in the living room portion of the space, fiddling with the tinsel on the mantle. There was a loud banging sound, followed by a few curse words. Finally, biting back a smile, she asked, "Can I help with anything?"

After what had to have been a solid thirty seconds, the man replied, "No."

Well. Kelly looked around the open concept living area, feeling awkward to say the least. So this guy was the caretaker, she supposed that explained why he was so curious in her being on the driveway. It did not, however, explain why it had not been plowed.

"Did you know I was renting this cottage for three weeks?" she asked, considering the condition of the place upon her arrival.

"Yes," he said, to her surprise. "Guests are rare at this time of year."

From the looks of things, guests were rare at any time of the year. "I'm Kelly," she said.

He poked his head around the door. "I know."

Exasperated, she said, "And you are?"

"Noah. Noah Branson." He offered up this information almost begrudgingly, and disappeared behind the door once more.

Kelly wandered over to the front window, where dusk was quickly encroaching. "So, I was thinking of going into town for supplies, and I was wondering if the driveway was going to be cleared anytime soon?" Like, after the heat came back on?

Noah poked his head around the doorframe again, naked impatience on his face. "Have you looked out the window recently?"

"I'm looking out it now," she said, feeling her temper rise. "And I just opened the door to you, too."

"No use plowing with the snow still come down so hard," he said and disappeared again.

Kelly realized her jaw was hanging and closed her mouth firmly, biting back a few choice curse words of her own. Suddenly there was a clank and a hiss and Noah reappeared in the doorway, toolbox in hand, his head bent as he made for the door.

"So it's fixed?" Kelly glanced at the nearest radiator.

Noah grunted in response. Charming.

He opened the door, allowing a rush of icy wind to flood the room, which indeed had started to warm up, Kelly realized with relief. He stepped out onto the small covered porch and, almost forcefully, turned and looked at her. "I'm headed into town now if you needed those supplies."

Kelly blinked in surprise. Was he offering her a ride or offering to run her errands? She decided not to push it.

"Thanks," she said, wanting to say no as much as she wanted to say yes. The wind was howling and the snow was falling in thick wet flakes that seemed to coat every surface and tree branch, making them glisten. Ten minutes alone with this man was about as appealing as a trip to the dentist, but the thought of trudging through the snow and back again with grocery bags in fashion boots was worse.

She followed him to the truck, taking great care in locking the door behind her. She could have sworn she heard a snort, but when she glanced over her shoulder, his expression was blank. Still. Suspicious.

"Don't mind the mess," he said as he walked to the truck, tossing the toolbox in the back.

Kelly took her time. Now that her hands were free of luggage and she knew that she was about to climb into a warm, albeit messy, truck, she could take a moment to enjoy the beauty of her surroundings. She lifted her head and stuck out her tongue, feeling an icy cold, feather-light flake hit her tongue and then melt, so quickly she could barely process the feeling.

"This is just magical," she sighed.

Noah was standing behind the open driver's door, looking at her as if she were half-crazy, and Kelly felt her cheeks heat with embarrassment. "We should go before the storm gets worse."

She climbed in and closed the door after her, feeling the need to explain herself. "I've never been to Oyster Bay," she said. "I've never even left California, unless you count a trip to Mexico when I was seven. My parents aren't really into family vacations." She glanced at him, waiting for a response, but his eyes were on the road, his hands on the wheel, and his expression so impassive, she wondered if he'd heard her over the whirr of the heat that blasted from the vents on the dashboard.

She pulled off her knitted gloves and held her hands over the vents, smiling a little. "That's why I'm here, actually, to see my family?" Again, no reaction. Surely he would know Hannah and Evie, though. He was somewhere near Hannah's age bracket; she'd estimate him to be around thirty, give or take a year.

She studied his jaw, strong and firm, dusted with a hint of five o'clock shadow, and piercing blue eyes that were a nice contrast to his nut-brown hair. He wore no hat. No gloves either, she thought, glancing at the steering wheel, and those hands…

She looked away, feeling her cheeks heat again. So he had nice hands.

"Hannah and Evie Donovan are my sisters. Well, my half-sisters. Their dad used to be married to my mom. Well, our mom. And then, well…I hear the entire town knows how that story ended, so I'm sure you already know."

"I don't like to pay attention to town gossip," Noah ground out, keeping his eyes on the road.

"Oh. Well, anyway, I grew up in California with our mother and they grew up here, and it's actually my first time visiting them. Hannah came to live out west about eleven years ago, but she left over a year ago to go traveling and then she moved back here, but you probably know that, in a town this small. So now I'm here. And it's going to be the best Christmas ever."

He glanced at her sidelong, and she thought he may have cocked an eyebrow, too.

Well!

They drove the rest of the way in silence, not even the radio to keep them company, and eventually Kelly stopped trying to think of conversation. But as they rounded the corner and Main Street came alive before them, Kelly couldn't help it, she let out a whoop. Or a cry. Or, okay, judging by the way Noah slammed on the breaks and uttered a four-letter word loudly, it might have been more of a scream.

"Jesus!" He glared at her. "You could have had us killed. I thought something happened."

But something had happened, Kelly wanted to say, and despite the muttering of frustration as he turned back to the road, she couldn't stop smiling.

"Isn't it beautiful?" she said, smiling out the window. She looked over at him and his scowling face.

"What's beautiful?"

"This town!" As if she should have to spell it out! "The lights! Christmas! It's come alive!"

"I'm not really into that sort of thing," he said curtly, as he was pulling into a nearby parking space. The bumper of the truck stopped just short of a pile of snow that looked nearly tall enough to sled down.

"What part of it aren't you into?" she asked.

He killed the engine. "All of it."

She blinked at him. "You mean…you don't like Christmas?"

"Nope," he said as he popped the locks and opened the door.

"But, but…" Sure, Christmas had never been her mother's thing, but to adamantly dislike the holiday was something different. She scrambled out of the car, meeting Noah at the sidewalk. "But who doesn't like Christmas?"

"Me," he said. He looked over her head, jutting his chin."The Corner Market is right there, good for groceries. And if you need any odds and ends, there's the general store right next door. I'll meet you back at the car in twenty minutes," he said, not bothering to ask her if that would be enough time, but judging from the snow that continued to fall, who was she to argue? After all, she had never driven in the snow. In fact, back in San Francisco, she didn't drive at all. She didn't even own a car. Couldn't afford one if she wanted to now.

A familiar flicker of panic made her heart seize up for a moment, until she looked around her, and she realized there was a time and a place for panic and there was a time and place for… "Magic."

Noah shook his head, gave her the side-eye, and stalked away. She watched him for a moment, wondering what business he had to take care of in town, and then, deciding she frankly didn't care and that her own business was much more interesting, she walked through the doors of the Corner Market as they opened automatically for her, and all at once Christmas carols began to joyfully play.

She grinned and grabbed a nearby cart, pausing just for a moment in the doorway to take it all in. It was exactly as Hannah had described, only Hannah probably hadn't even realized when she casually mentioned the downtown of Oyster Bay, and the sole, small grocer that had such a cute name, that Kelly had been committing it all to memory, that she had longed to be there, standing in front of the cheese display, just like she now did.

Sure, to Hannah and Evie and no doubt every other person in this town it was just a cheese display, but to her...it was the opportunity to walk in her sisters' shoes for a moment, to imagine their everyday routine, to experience all the little things she'd missed. To know them.

Well, sure, of course she knew Hannah. But all that time she'd spent with Hannah, Kelly had been painfully aware of this other life her sister had, the one Kelly had never known, the one that Hannah always referred to as "home".

She glanced behind her, out the window, wondering if the school pageant could possibly still be going on in this weather! But as she strolled the aisles, taking her time to stop and smile at Mr. Novak, who baked the best croissants other than Angie's (the very café that Kelly would be dining at tomorrow morning), and who gave her a quizzical look of the "Do we know each other?" caliber but then grinned anyway.

Maybe he noticed that she resembled Hannah. They both had their mother's coloring. Dark eyes and hair, unlike the fair Evie, who favored her father.

It made Kelly nervous to think about tiptoeing around the subject of their mother with Evie. And when Kelly got nervous, or depressed, she did one thing every time. She hit the frozen foods section. Immediately, her favorite comfort foods were lined up in front of her. Fried cheese sticks and pizzas and ice cream and...nope, not going to do it. Now wasn't the time to wallow or dwell. She'd come to Oyster Bay to break that cycle. To do something good for herself.

There was a microwave at the cottage and an oven, and she grabbed all the ingredients she would need to bake cookies with her sisters. She could just picture them standing at the (albeit small) counter, stirring batter and telling stories and drinking wine. Wine! Yes, she would grab that, too, after she finished adding some peppermint stick ice cream and frozen appetizers to her cart. Her stomach grumbled and she suddenly remembered she hadn't eaten yet today, unless you counted the pretzels they handed out on the flight. Tonight she'd watch a Christmas movie, eat a frozen pizza, and prepare for tomorrow. And knit. Yes, knitting always calmed her.

She was just adding some mixed nuts to her cart (she'd put them out in small dishes, even if they were of the paper variety, they were at least seasonally themed, ever the perfect hostess) when Noah came up behind her and cleared his throat. Loudly.

"Jesus!" she said, holding a hand to her heart.

"Now you know how it feels," he said, but there was a hint of amusement in his eyes as he looked down at her cart. "You've been busy."

"Well, there's a snowstorm out there, and I'm expecting guests this weekend," she said primly.

He cocked an eyebrow. Okay, he was sort of cute. His eyes were sparkling in an almost friendly way, or maybe that was the reflection of the tinsel coming off the twinkling lights that were roped around the ceiling. Yes, she'd go with that theory.

"I'm almost finished," she said, thinking of the chocolate covered pretzels she'd spotted in aisle three, but the look of impatience he gave her made her change her mind. Besides, there was always tomorrow. By then, the snow would probably have melted and she and her sisters might spend the day in town, Christmas shopping. She nearly laughed out loud with sheer joy.

And she might have, judging from the strange expression that came over Noah's face.

"Right," she said, jutting her chin and gripping the handle of her cart. "I'll just, er, check out."

"I'll be in the truck," he announced, much to her relief. Honestly! There was something about him that made her uneasy, and it wasn't just the broody temperament and textbook good looks.

"Don't see much of Noah around here," the cashier said as Kelly finished loading her items onto the counter. She tucked a strand of silvering hair behind her ear and reached for the bottles of wine, which she slid into brown paper sleeves. "Usually he has his items delivered."

"I wouldn't know," Kelly said a little apologetically. "I'm just visiting."

"Just visiting and you already got to know the town's biggest Scrooge?" The woman looked at her in wonder, and Kelly felt her curiosity pique. Without needing to ask, the woman leaned in and said, "Rarely comes into town, that one. And when he does, you can bet he's not talking to anyone. Barely makes eye contact, too. It's a shame, really, he was the sweetest little boy. Knew him all his life. Or…most of it." The woman stiffened when a man wearing a tie walked by and gave her a stern look.

"Brown bags or paper, dear?" the woman said with a bright smile.

"Paper," Kelly said absentmindedly.

She was still thinking about what the woman had said when she made her way to the truck, exhaust pouring out of the engine pipe as she approached. Noah was buckled in, the radio on, talk radio again, his head back against the seat.

"I didn't have a chance to get any towels," Kelly remembered.

"There are some in the chest at the foot of the bed," he replied, shifting the gear into reverse. They drove in silence, the radio keeping them company, the view a winter wonderland that kept Kelly's mind from drifting to the broody guy beside her, at least not too much, and when they reached the cottage, Noah hopped out of the truck to pull the grocery bags from the back.

"You know, you should really tack that shutter in place before the wind snaps it off," she remarked as she set a bag at the base of the porch. Almost to prove her point, the loose piece began banging against the siding.

He shrugged. "Don't see the point in sinking much money into it. It's going to be torn down in the spring, once the ground thaws."

"Torn down?" She looked at the small house that was now her home, at least for the next three weeks, and felt heart sink. Today was just the beginning, and he was already confirming an end to the experience. "But—"

But he had already turned to go. She stood in the doorway, watching him walk to the truck, and then, with a heavy heart, turned back to the front porch, that was admittedly in need of repair.

Well, so much for asking Noah for any help. If he didn't intend to take care of the place, she'd just handle it herself.

*

Noah stood in the front bay window of the "big house"; at least that's what he'd always called it as a kid. It was a quarter of a mile up the hill, through the wrought iron gates that divided it from the rest of the world, set it apart. Back when he was a kid, he thought the "big house" was something haunted, a little mysterious, with secret passageways and doors.

It had its share of secrets, all right, he thought wryly. Just not the ones you wanted to discover. Oh, there was gossip. Of course his mother's behavior couldn't be hidden, no matter how much Gran and Gramps tried to smooth it over, save face. But the rest of it, what happened behind closed doors, was closely guarded.

And best forgotten.

He turned from the window, only because Murphy was pawing at his leg, wanting to go out. He'd already devoured the gourmet dog food Noah had stocked up on in town tonight, in case the forecast was wrong and the storm didn't move south by morning, and the roads were too bad for deliveries. He'd left work early, just to be sure he got to the store in time. He supposed there were some perks that came with being the big boss.

But not enough.

"Okay, bud, follow me." He gave the mutt a scratch behind the ears and they walked side by side down the hallway to the front door, where Murphy's red leash was hanging on the coat rack. Maybe it was crazy to even bother with the leash, considering the grounds were expansive and fenced in, along with the noticeable fact that Murphy was rarely more than two feet from his side, but once a runner always a runner, and Noah wasn't taking any chances.

The people at Heartland Shelter told him that Murphy had been found wandering behind a gas station, no collar or chip, no missing signs that matched his description. A runaway, most likely. And Noah was keenly aware of the risk that it could happen again.

Patterns rarely broke, he'd learned that the hard way, and early on in life, too.

The snow was deep, but Murphy didn't mind. He dashed through it with the energy of a puppy, his mouth pulled into a grin, his tail wagging.

Noah grinned. "Over here, Murph." He didn't know why he was whispering. The land stretched between him and the cottage, once belonging to the caretaker's family before he and his mother took residency.

Still, it was a quiet night. So quiet you could hear the wind snapping the tree branches.

He pulled the leash closer, leading Murphy to a path that had been shielded by tall pines and only lightly dusted in snow.

With the tree limbs bare of their leaves, he had a clear view of the cottage, lit from within, Kelly barely visible as she passed through the small, cramped rooms. Suddenly, the door flung open, and she appeared, disappeared around the back of the house for a moment, and reappeared with an armful of firewood, kindling that must have been a dozen years old and was probably soaked all the way through, if it hadn't rotted yet.

He frowned, wondering what she could be doing, and then watched as she struggled to carry the wood back in, the rickety door slamming shut behind her. It took a solid ten minutes for the smoke to start pouring out of the chimney and he could only hope that she'd had the sense to open the flue. The chimney hadn't been serviced in years. He supposed he should have removed that bit about the wood-burning fireplace from the description in the ad, but then, how else was he supposed to lure anybody in? He could hardly point out the real facts, like the bad furnace and the unreliable water tank, or the other parts of the cottage that went deeper than surface level, that made him hate the look of the place and want to turn his back away from the view. Only he couldn't.

He could only sit and watch and think about the pretty young woman who was sitting down there all by herself, lighting a fire, no doubt singing Christmas carols and proclaiming the experience to be "magical."

A slow smile crept up his face, but he set his jaw quickly.

Kelly Myers might find that cottage to be something special, but he didn't. Never could, never would.

With any luck she'd spare him the trouble of tearing it down and burn it to the ground instead, he thought wryly. And then, he did smile.

Chapter Three

The next morning, Kelly woke to the sound of silence. For a moment, the world was so still that she wondered if this was all just a dream. But then she wiggled her toes under the thick, patchwork quilt, that must have been handmade by someone at some point in time, and smiled. It wasn't a dream. She was in Oyster Bay. And today she was finally going to meet Evie.

She showered and dressed and made coffee, and then settled with her mug onto the window seat in the living room that lent a view of the wood-lined path that led to the main road. She frowned, noticing that someone had plowed it, and she wondered idly if it was Noah, or if there was a service for that kind of thing.

Given the Grinch he was turning out to be, she had to assume it was the work of a good Samaritan, or at least a paid service.

The snow had let up, leaving a winter wonderland in its wake. Tree branches were frocked with snow, and all around her, the world seemed to glisten. She reached over and flicked on the radio which was set to the Christmas station and closed her eyes. This was it. Her best Christmas yet. And it started today.

Her stomach began to flutter with nerves, but she pushed them back into place. After all, her sisters had invited her here, even offered up their homes, and besides, it wasn't like she hadn't spoken to Evie before. On the contrary, they now texted fairly often, and they were up to date on their current lives and recent struggles: Brian cheating on her with her so-called friend; losing a job that she didn't even like over her inability to get over Brian; and her recent reestablishment of her love for knitting.

She glanced at the clock, anxiety kicking up a notch. She was scheduled to meet her sisters at Angie's Café at ten, and she estimated that it would take her at least fifteen minutes to walk there, meaning she should probably leave, well…now.

She took her time washing her mug and drying it with a paper towel. Would it be better to be sitting, waiting, or better to walk in, once they were already settled? Of course it would be natural and wonderful to see Hannah. Sure, it had been a while, but there was no awkwardness there. But Evie…Would she look like her pictures?

Would she look at all like her? Evie resembled her father. Blue eyes and fair hair, but surely there would be a hint of their lineage in there, some connection to the woman who was mother to them all?

No better way to find out than to go. And she would. Once the next Christmas carol had finished playing. She wasn't procrastinating. It was her favorite. A sure sign that she should wait. Be the last to arrive. The universe had handed her the answer, and she would let it be her guide. After all, she didn't have any one else to ask. If her mother knew that she had come here, to Oyster Bay… Well, there was no telling what she would do.

*

Kelly had already drained half her peppermint mocha when the door to Angie's opened again, the happy bells chiming a new arrival, and just like they had the last three times, she jumped.

But it was just two middle-aged women bundled in down parkas, their hair covered in thick wool hats that matched their scarves. Kelly slumped back in her seat and checked her phone, wondering if Hannah had left a message or if she'd gotten the time wrong. She was just about to call her sister and find out for herself when she felt a tap at her shoulder and she looked up to see Hannah grinning down at her. Relief swept over her as quickly as the anxiety built. Her eyes darted from Hannah to the woman next to her. A woman who only slightly resembled her photos, a woman whose nose was a bit more upturned than the image she'd built in her mind, whose almond-shaped eyes were kind but uncertain, whose hair had clearly been trimmed since her byline photo was taken, and whose smile was…exactly like her mother's. *Their* mother's.

Oh my God, this was her sister. Kelly stood, awkwardly, the chair making a painful dragging sound when she pushed it back against the wood floors, and hugged Hannah. Together again, after nearly two years! But it wasn't Hannah she was thinking about right now. It was this other person, the sister who had been right by Hannah's side all those years, who stood loyally at her side right now as if they were family members greeting a distant cousin.

She pulled away from Hannah as the jealousy reared fierce and ugly, knowing there was no point in it, that Hannah hadn't kept Evie from her all those years. But rather, that Evie had stayed away.

"I can't believe it's you," Evie said. Her voice was soft, soothing, and sweet, and Kelly was having one of those surreal moments again, just like yesterday when the cab driver had rounded the corner and Main Street had popped up all around her.

"I can't believe I'm here," she said, glancing at Hannah for reassurance, but it was Evie who leaned forward and embraced her. Not stiffly, the way Loraine would have done, but rather, well, honestly, was the only word that came to Kelly's mind.

"I wish I hadn't waited so long," Evie said when she stepped back. Her face was lined with regret, and for that one, brief moment, all those years of hurt and rejection disappeared.

"Well, we have today," Hannah said brightly. "And this is just the first of many visits, I hope?"

"Absolutely!" Kelly dropped back into her chair, her nervous energy replaced with excitement. She reached into her bag and pulled out her list.

"What's that?" Evie seemed to laugh as she saw the numbered list, typed and printed, and yes, maybe decorated with a few holiday themed stickers she'd found in the back of a junk drawer. Unemployment could be boring, after all.

Hannah was leaning forward with interest as she pulled her hat off and set it on the table. Kelly felt her cheeks flush as she looked down at the paper. As an only child (well, not technically, but that's how it had felt) she was used to being the center of attention, the kid facing the two adults, and it suddenly felt that way again, with her sisters on the opposite side of the table, both giving her their full interest.

"It's a list of all the things we can do together while I'm here," she said.

Evie grinned. "I like that idea. What do you have?"

Kelly didn't need to refer to the list. She had it all memorized by heart. She'd been gathering the memories that Hannah had shared, tucking them away, inserting herself in the scene, imagining herself there. And now she was.

"Seems like a good day to go sledding on Shell Hill," she said.

Evie and Hannah were still for a moment, until Hannah burst out laughing. "*Sledding*?"

Kelly frowned at her sister, wondering what was suddenly the big deal. When she was in California she talked about her sledding afternoons as if they were the most fantastic experiences that she couldn't wait to get back to. "You told me how much you loved sledding."

"When I was a kid!" Hannah shook her head and slurped for her coffee.

Evie's forehead was creased as she looked at Kelly. "I haven't been sledding in years. It might be fun. It's kind of cold though…"

She was only saying it to be nice, that much was clear, but oh, how Kelly loved her for it. Loved it so much that she suddenly missed Evie more than ever, even though she was sitting right here, close enough to touch. She'd been missing Evie all her life, just like she'd been missing stupid things, like sledding on that toboggan, and now, well now she knew more than ever just what she had been missing. This town. The Christmas spirit. All the things that her sisters now seemed to take for granted, even Hannah, who knew just how different the holidays were in California…

"What else is on the list?" Evie asked.

Kelly felt uncomfortable now, and she folded it in half,

and in half again. "It's not important," she said.

Evie nudged Hannah, hard, and Hannah reached out to grab the list, but Kelly snatched it away just in time. "Let me see it," Hannah urged. When Kelly tried to stuff it into the front pocket of her handbag, Hannah reached over the table, and Kelly used her body to shield the bag altogether, causing Hannah to nearly spill her coffee.

"Jesus, we're acting like children!" Evie said, but she was laughing, and Kelly was too, she realized. She didn't care if they were acting like kids. This was exactly what she'd longed for.

"It feels good," Kelly admitted.

Hannah gave a small grin. "It does. And this is exactly why I wanted you to stay with me."

Kelly shook her head. "You and Dan are just now back together."

"And it's as if no time has passed." Hannah set her coffee down. "Sort of like this. Only this is better. You. Here. No Loraine."

Kelly glanced at Evie who was staring at the table, her expression tight. And there it was. Evie had never met their mother, well, not when she was old enough to remember her. Loraine had left Chip and Oyster Bay when Evie was just a baby, and Kelly was living proof of why Evie had been abandoned.

She knew she shouldn't feel guilty, that she hadn't chosen to be born, after all, and that Evie was understanding enough to see this, but judging by the expression on her sister's face, the issue was still sore.

"Still not in touch with her then?" she asked, even though it was pretty obvious. Hannah and Loraine hadn't exactly bonded during the time her sister lived in California, and Kelly knew that when Hannah left town, she wouldn't be returning any time soon.

Hannah shook her head. "I tried, and maybe someday I'll try again. At least I can say I have no regrets."

Evie picked up her mug and sipped it. Did she have regrets? Kelly didn't know and was afraid to ask.

"Well, I'm fine at the cottage," Kelly said, eager to get off the subject of their mother.

"Cottage?" Now it was Hannah's turn to frown. "You told me you were staying at the Oyster Bay Hotel."

That had been the original plan, yes, but the Oyster Bay Hotel was way out of her budget, and Hannah still didn't know about her lack of employment. It wasn't that Kelly had wanted to keep the news from her sister, but it wasn't exactly something to brag about either.

But Evie. Evie knew the truth. And now she gave Kelly a little wink of camaraderie, a nudge that it would be okay to admit her recent failures, that maybe, everything would be okay in general. "I'm actually sort of…in a transition period."

Hannah's frown deepened. "What do you mean?"

"Well, I'm not at the real estate firm anymore," Kelly said, struggling to make eye contact. She couldn't help it. She felt the need to please Hannah, to keep her happy, to keep her, well, close.

"Good!" Hannah said, to her surprise, but then she realized, of course, Hannah always had her back, from the time she appeared in her life up until the day she left it. Or rather, up until the day she moved back to Oyster Bay. Now, Kelly realized with both shame and relief that Hannah was still on her side, even though she hadn't been in the physical sense for a while. "You are way too creative to be spending your time analyzing commercial real estate trends in office buildings!"

It was true, and Hannah of all people could relate, being a photographer and someone who was determined to follow her passion. She glanced at Evie, knowing that the creative bone was not exactly shared by their other sister. But Evie seemed to take no offense. Instead she nodded and said, "Sometimes life has a strange way of guiding you to the place you were meant to be. I'm a shining example. After all, I didn't get the job I thought I wanted and ended up realizing my true calling wasn't working in a hospital with patients, but rather, writing an advice column."

"Have you thought about what you'll do next?" Hannah asked.

Kelly shook her head. She hadn't, not really, and just admitting that to herself made her heart race with anxiety. The jobs she'd applied for were out of necessity—paying work, and work she knew she wouldn't love. "I'm hoping to figure that while I'm in town. The hotel was too pricey, and the cottage felt like a better option for a long-term stay anyway." After all, a hotel didn't come with a fireplace or a living room with space for a Christmas tree or a kitchen for baking cookies. Staying in a hotel for Christmas would be just as depressing as, well, being home for Christmas.

"What cottage are you referring to?" Evie asked. "Most rental properties around here come with huge price tags!"

"Not this one," Kelly said, meeting her sisters' quizzical exchange. "It's just down the street. In the woods. Noah Branson is the caretaker…"

Now it was Evie's turn to choke on her coffee, and Hannah's eyes had gone wide as saucers. Kelly looked from each sister to the next, registering their mutual horror. "What? What is it?"

"You cannot be telling me you are staying at the White Pine Cottage," Hannah said firmly.

"Oh, that's right! The name! That probably would have been a better way to identify it," Kelly said mildly, but her sisters were still staring at her, and she suddenly felt like she had done something very wrong. "Why, what's wrong with it?"

"Noah Branson took over the property," Evie started to explain.

"And that's the problem with it," Hannah finished.

Kelly wasn't convinced. Noah was grumpy and a little hard to read, but he wasn't exactly unfriendly. "You two are overreacting," Kelly said, waving a hand through the air. It did warm her heart to think that they were being overprotective of her, though. What she would have given to have that opportunity growing up? Two sisters that she could confide in when Loraine was doing her usual unsupportive mom act. Three allies to have each other's back, to keep each other's secrets, and fight each other's battles. If only. "The way you two are staring at me, you'd think he was an axe murderer or something!"

Hannah lifted an eyebrow. "You never know. Does that cottage have a basement? I wouldn't want to go down the stairs and see what's down there."

Evie laughed, but now Kelly was feeling a little bit wary. "What is so wrong with him? When he drove me into town last night, he was perfectly fine." Fine might not be the best word choice, she thought. More like edgy, broody, and a little mysterious.

Painfully attractive. And wrong, all wrong! What she needed was a sweet, affable guy who was happy to be at her side, and never leave it.

Correction: what she needed was no guy at all. What she needed was a job. Security. To settle into her adult life once and for all.

"You got in the car with him?" Hannah's eyes were so round that Kelly could see the whites all around them.

"Well, I couldn't exactly walk to the grocery store in that weather!" Kelly laughed.

"I wish you had called me. I would have taken you." Evie smiled at her, and for that one, heart-wrenching moment, Kelly wished she had called Evie. Sure, Hannah had been busy, but why hadn't she called her other sister?

They could have used that time to bond, have some alone time, get to know each other, tell each other all the little parts of their lives that the other hadn't been there to witness.

But she knew why she hadn't called Evie. "I guess I wasn't sure what it would be like. Meeting after all this time." She shrugged, and Evie nodded her head a little sadly.

"Wait, I'm not done talking about your accommodations. Or your little friendship with Noah Branson." Hannah all but hissed the last sentence of her remark. "Kelly, he's…he's…well, he's not someone you should invest too much time in. He's cold. Some might even say he's heartless."

Evie scrunched up her nose. "I have to agree. He's very reclusive and not very friendly. He has issues. Really, he should probably write me a letter. Or ten. I'd be happy to help him."

"If he could be helped," Hannah snorted.

Issues? Kelly was curious about just what they were referring to, but she was equally eager to get off the topic of her stay at the White Pine Cottage, and her reason for not staying at somewhere her sisters found to be more suitable. Every time she thought of her lack of employment, the cost of this trip, and the lack of prospects waiting her back in San Francisco, she felt like she might be sick.

"What's the plan for your column?" Kelly asked, and

Evie sighed, shrugging off the question as she fought a smile.

She was humble. Reserved but kind. All the ways that Kelly had imagined her to be only, dare she say, better? Even though she was younger than Hannah, there was an old soul there. Someone who took care of people, saw into their deeper thoughts, not just the ones that they openly revealed.

But there was another side of her, Kelly knew. The one who had refused to support Hannah's decision to meet their mother—and her. The one who had never visited California in all those years. The one who had never initiated contact with Kelly, and who might never have, if Kelly hadn't taken it upon herself a few months ago.

That stung. But that was something she had vowed not to focus on. Not on this first day, when they had come so far.

"Liam said her column will be featured in over fifty newspapers around the country," Hannah said proudly, and Kelly couldn't fight the sting when she saw the light in her sister's eyes. It was the same way she described Evie all those years ago, when they were sitting at a juice bar, or sometimes in her old childhood bedroom, talking for hours, the way sisters did, and no matter how close they were and no matter how much they had in common, there was never going to be any competing with Evie.

"When will I meet Liam?" Kelly wanted to know. "And Dan! And Lucy." She had tucked away that pom-

pom hat, just for the girl.

"Tomorrow's the party at the inn," Evie said.

"You'll get to meet the entire family," Hannah added.

"Well, *your* family," Kelly pointed out. After all, the Harper cousins were of no relation to her or their mother. Bridget, Margo, and Abby's mother had been Chip's sister. Kelly wasn't part of that clan.

"Our family is your family," Hannah insisted, as she had always done, so eager to settle any concern, to bring Kelly into the fold. And she had, mostly. "What should we do after this?"

There was still the list of traditions that she didn't seem too excited about revisiting. Or Evie. She had wanted to invite them both over to her cottage to bake cookies this afternoon, but now that no longer felt like such a good idea.

So much for sledding on Shell Hill, Kelly thought, with a pang in her chest. She considered offering up one of the other items she'd longed to try (snowman building, or caroling off-key as Hannah claimed they'd been forced to do, door to door, by Mimi, the Harper cousins' grandmother, the five little girls all dressed in matching red coats).

But they weren't little girls anymore, and Kelly hadn't been the sixth in the mix.

"I have some last-minute shopping to do," Evie offered.

Kelly smiled with more enthusiasm than she felt. So

her sisters wanted to go shopping. That would be fun. Ordinary, but fun.

And wasn't that what she'd longed for? An ordinary day with her sisters. Here, in magical Oyster Bay.

*

The first place they hit was Bayside Brides. "Should I know something you haven't shared?" Kelly asked as Hannah's eyes lit up at the window display: a beautiful snowy scene with an ivory lace gown dusted in what must have been tens of thousands of tiny crystals.

"Hardly," Hannah said. "But Lucy saw a tiara in the window one day and I wanted to get it for her for Christmas."

"I got a tiara for Christmas once," Kelly mused. "I must have been about four and I was going through a princess phase. You know." But both Hannah and Evie looked at her with head tilts and half smiles, as if they didn't know, of course they didn't, but that they were happy to hear.

Right. So maybe they weren't into that kind of thing. Hannah had portrayed their childhood to be more of the tomboy variety: uncombed hair, showers in the outside stall behind the house, long days at the beach and long nights on the tree swing in the backyard. They'd been raised by a single dad without a woman's touch. Not that Loraine could classify as maternal. Still, she knew how to pick out clothes and do hair, and once in a while, she even cooked dinner, something of the organic variety, and then there had been that vegan phase. Loraine was always trying to find herself. It was, Kelly now understood, the reason that she had left Oyster Bay. But all these years later, she was still searching, searching through clubs, groups, hobbies. Men. Her three daughters weren't enough to keep her satisfied, painful as it was to admit.

"Anyway," she said, with a shrug, "let's get inside. I'm freezing."

They pushed through the door, which jingled bells announcing their arrival, and Hannah immediately fell into conversation with a pretty blonde woman with bright blue eyes.

"That's our friend Sarah Preston," Evie informed her. "She used to work at the paper, but now she works here." Perhaps sensing Kelly's anxiety at remembering these details, and trying to place the stories, she grinned. "Don't worry. By this time next week, you'll know the whole town."

Kelly felt her shoulders relax. She liked that idea. A lot, in fact.

"Sarah, this is my sister," Hannah said, as Kelly and Evie approached.

Sarah looked at Evie and back at Hannah, her brow knitting. "Um, yeah, I know. We worked together for a few months. I was at your house for Thanksgiving, too."

"I mean my other sister," Hannah clarified. Her *other* sister. God, how Kelly hated that term.

"Her *youngest* sister," Kelly said, stepping forward. She extended her hand. "Kelly Myers."

"Kelly!" Now Sarah's eyes were round and Kelly wasn't so sure she would ever blink again. She glanced at Hannah and back again. "I see the resemblance!"

Kelly beamed. She and Hannah did look like sisters, and they'd bonded like sisters, too. But Evie, she thought, looking over…Evie was all Chip.

Except for that smile. Evie probably didn't even realize she had their mother's smile. Hannah had apparently hung onto a photo of Loraine when she was younger, until she reached an age where she realized their mother wasn't coming back, and supposedly smashed the frame. After that, Chip had packed up all the memories of Loraine and stored them in the attic. Something told Kelly that Evie had never dug them out.

"How long are you in town for?" Sarah asked.

"Three weeks," Kelly said. "I leave the day after New Year's." She realized with regret that she didn't want to leave, that she had nothing to look forward to, no job to return to, and that her life suddenly felt wide open and well, empty. At least this past month she'd had this trip to keep her focused and optimistic, but now, her future suddenly seemed bleak. What was waiting for her in San Francisco? A boyfriend who had run off with her so-called-friend, Shannon? A father who traveled too often for work? A mother whose monthly dinners now centered around dodging the topic of her affair with a yoga instructor named Chaz?

Loraine didn't even know she was here right now. Really, that was for the best.

"You're coming to the party tomorrow, right?" Evie asked Sarah, as Hannah went off to the display of tiaras, each so sparkly that even Kelly was drawn to them.

"Of course. I bought a new dress just for the occasion!"

Hannah set down the first tiara and turned to Sarah. "You do know that there will be no surprise guests at this party."

"Well, maybe some guests from the inn…"

Hannah shook her head. "Do you think many single men are staying at a romantic country inn two weeks before Christmas?"

Sarah's shoulders slumped. "You're right. You're right. It's impossible to find a handsome, available man in a town this small!"

Kelly wondered if Noah Branson was technically unavailable or if he was just that undesirable. His good looks and age bracket would imply he should be high on someone like Sarah's list, but after what her sisters had said, maybe that wasn't the case.

"Why do I bother?" Sarah said. Turning to Kelly, she asked, "Do you have a boyfriend?"

Kelly sighed inwardly. "Not anymore."

Unlike the look of sympathy that Evie gave her, Sarah's face broke into a huge smile. "Excellent. I have a feeling we will be fast friends."

Kelly liked the sound of this. And she liked the fact that Sarah was going to be at the party tomorrow. She needed all the friendly faces she could get right now, especially if… "So who all will be at the party?" She'd been afraid to ask, but now she needed to know, to prepare herself.

"Oh, Bridget and Jack and Emma of course," Evie said, referring to the innkeeper herself, her new husband and her young daughter. Kelly knew all about Bridget's first marriage and how her ex now ran a pub in town that the girls actively boycotted out of loyalty to their eldest cousin.

They were loyal that way, Kelly now realized. Forsaking all else in the name of family. And somehow she had fallen on enemy territory, in the Loraine camp, in the homewrecker camp, on the side that wasn't on Chip's side.

"And Margo and Eddie and Abby and Zach. Mimi and Earl. Our dad, of course."

So there it was. Chip was coming. Secretly, Kelly had been hoping he'd be working all day, seeing as he ran a restaurant. "He can take the day off work then?" She tried to keep her tone casual, but it came out tight and strangled.

"For a few hours," Hannah said, grinning over her shoulder.

Kelly studied her sisters, who were happily perusing the shop, listening to Sarah chatter on about the newest inventory of faux fur stoles, then adding with a heavy sigh, "Of course, it's tempting to try all this stuff on, but I'm not in a position to tempt fate with my dating track record."

"Oh, Sarah," Evie said, setting a hand on her shoulder.

Kelly stared at a display of costume jewelry, but her mind was spinning and she could barely even process what she was looking at. It seemed that no one thought anything about Chip and Kelly being in the same room tomorrow. Except Kelly. Kelly thought about it a lot. She thought what Chip would think. She thought what Loraine would think.

And she wondered how she would feel, seeing the man who sounded like the kind of parent she could have only ever dreamed of having for herself.

Sure, Evie might have thought she'd been short-changed all those years ago, but she had no idea just how good she had it.

Chapter Four

The Harper House Inn was everything Hannah had described it to be, and more. As they pulled into the driveway, Kelly took in the sight of the old, Victorian house, set back from the road by a gravel driveway, the front yard a blanket of snow and the backyard showing just a glimpse of the sea where foamy waves crashed against the rocky shore. Wreaths of fresh pine were hung from every window by red ribbons, and garland was wrapped around the front porch posts. A single candle was placed on every sill, and even though it was midafternoon, the sky was overcast, and the lights were bright and welcoming.

"This is going to be fun!" Lucy said from the backseat they shared. Hannah and Dan were up front. He was just as dreamy as Hannah had painted him out to be, and after years of listening to Hannah talk about him, and then not talk about him, or at least talk about him with trying not to, she felt as if she already knew him. At the very least, she probably knew much more about him than he knew she did, she thought with a little smile.

"Too bad my dad can't make it," Hannah said as she released her seatbelt. "He was asked to cater a holiday party at the last minute."

Kelly hoped the relief didn't show in her face as she opened the door and stepped outside, the snow crunching under the soles of her boots.

"Another time," she said, knowing that she couldn't dodge the inevitable much longer. She was eager to meet Chip, and how couldn't she be? Chip had made Hannah and Evie pancakes for breakfast on weekends when they were growing up. He had installed a tree swing in the backyard. He had ferried them to dance class and come to all their recitals. The man was a superstar. He was both revered and adored.

And somehow he hadn't been enough. Somehow Hannah had still felt the urge to fly out west and meet her and Loraine.

When she heard the stories about Hannah's childhood, she didn't even understand how that was possible. And every moment that she spent in Oyster Bay made her even more perplexed by it.

She pulled in a breath as she followed Dan and Hannah up the stairs to the front porch, the flutter in her stomach growing with each step she took. This was the house that her sisters had spent many afternoons in, baking cookies with their dad's sister and playing charades and hide and go seek and dress-up in the attic with their three cousins. The Harper sisters. For so many years they felt like folklore, the girls who had become more like sisters to Hannah and Evie than she had been.

It was Margo who greeted them at the door. She had a kind, open smile, and a glow in her cheeks that seemed to stem from pure joy. Or too much punch. But Kelly was assuming it was the first impression. She knew from Hannah how Margo had just returned to Oyster Bay a little over a year ago, after a failed marriage to her college boyfriend. Now she was happily married to her high school sweetheart, running her own interior design business in town, and helping out at the inn when Bridget needed an extra set of hands.

"You look so much like Hannah," Margo said to her, and reached out to embrace her before Kelly could protest, not that she wanted to. She was in the fold! Literally! Part of the Harper family home for Christmas. The stuff of late-night stories not too many years ago. And now it was here, real, the smells, sights, and the people. "Here, let me take your coat."

Kelly shrugged out of the wool peacoat and handed it to Margo, who eyed it in alarm. "You'll freeze to death in this. Bridget probably has one she can lend you before you go. She's about your size."

Turning at the sound of her name, a pretty, blonde

woman with her hair pulled back in a low ponytail walked over with her hand extended. "We've heard so much about you since Hannah moved back."

Kelly shook Bridget's hand and glanced at Hannah. Had she really shared so much? Like the fact that she and Loraine had never really connected the way that Hannah had hoped, and that eventually Hannah had given up, moved on, leaving Kelly behind and lonelier than ever?

"All good, I hope," she joked.

"Of course," Hannah hung her coat in the closet, not waiting to be asked, and no one lunged to help her, either. A sure sign of familiarity.

"Well, except that time that you and your mom got in that big fight, and you locked yourself in your bedroom, and the doorknob fell off!" Lucy's eyes were alive with mischief, and it took Kelly a moment to even remember what she was talking about.

But of course, one of Kelly's many teenage moments, when she and Loraine were at war, usually over something that wasn't the real source of the problem at all. Sometimes, she realized looking back, she provoked her mother on purpose, just to get a reaction, just to get…well, something, she supposed.

That time she had been upset over missing a party at her then best friend Lana's house. Loraine was having a few ladies from her organic cooking club over for wine and she needed Kelly to play hostess, a role Kelly had been very familiar with as Loraine flitted through clubs (self-help book club, meditation circle, feng shui group, vegan lifestyle club, and once, poker group). Loraine threw herself into whatever caught her interest at the moment…until it faded.

She supposed it was no different with relationships. She was hot for Chip and then she was not. And recently, and perhaps not so recently, Kelly thought uneasily, she'd gone cold on Kelly's father, too.

"How long were you stuck in your room?" Dan asked, clearly delighted with the story, or perhaps eager for information, lest he and sweet little Lucy have a drag out fight like that one someday.

Kelly eyed the girl. Nope. Not possible. She was too sweet, and Dan seemed far too level-headed and laidback to rock the relationship.

"Until Hannah figured out how to reattach the doorknob," Kelly said. "My mother was too busy tending to her guests to deal with it."

She caught Hannah's eye, and they exchanged a resigned but knowing smile, and just like that, all was right with the world again. It had helped, all those years, having Hannah on her side, knowing that someone was there, someone got it, someone understood.

"Why don't you go find Emma before you decide to start telling more stories," Hannah told Lucy.

"She was over near the dessert table the last time I checked," Bridget said, pride showing in her smile when she spotted her daughter, Hannah and Evie's first cousin once removed. No relation to Kelly, she reminded herself.

But still...she saw a resemblance. Not to Hannah, but to Evie. Both were fair haired, like Bridget. Like Chip. Like his sister.

Hannah and Evie's aunt had taken Loraine's place, Kelly knew. She'd taken them shopping for back to school clothes, baked cookies with them at Christmas, had "the talk," and kept an eye on the school calendar and on Chip, too. Kelly had never known any other family. She had no aunts or uncles or cousins. When her aunt died, Hannah's grief was a mystery to Kelly, something she couldn't touch, something she wasn't a part of. Now, seeing this house, feeling the warmth, the love, the connection, now she understood.

This house, even if it was now an inn and open to the public, was a home. A real family home.

She took in the room. The overstuffed sofas and chairs with soft, chunky throws in shades of ivory and soft greens, and the candles that flickered on the coffee tables in their mercury glass votives. Logs crackled in the fireplace, and the mantle contained family photos of Christmases past, happy memories captured forever in time.

Back at her childhood home, everything was white. White and, well, cold.

"I wish I had room for you here," Bridget said with an apologetic smile. "I can't believe we're actually booked through the next three months!"

"I'm not surprised," Kelly said, looking around the beautiful house. The living room was painted in warm, coastal colors with overstuffed couches and armchairs and thick ivory throws. The tables were in warm wood tones that matched the hardwood floors, and the rugs were plush and colorful. "It's absolutely beautiful."

"Well, I have my sister Margo to thank for that," Bridget admitted. "She's an interior designer. I was in real estate before I started the inn."

"I used to work in real estate," Kelly said, happy to find a link with this woman. "But now I'm, well, between jobs."

"Were you happy in your old job?" Bridget led them farther into the room and waved at a few people along the way.

"No," Kelly admitted.

Bridget grinned. "Then you have something to look forward to. This is a temporary phase. You'll get through it."

"Hey, I have an idea!" Hannah's face lit up as she grabbed a glass of eggnog from a tray set out on a console table. "You should sell some of your items at the Christmas Bazaar."

"That's an excellent idea," Evie agreed. She shook her head when Hannah held out a glass of the drink to her. "It's next Saturday. Everyone in town goes. And it sounds like you've been knitting a lot!"

Sell some of her items? Kelly had to admit that it was something she had thought about before, but only in passing. Her mother had supported the decision, strangely more than she had supported her job as a research analyst for the commercial real estate firm she'd been fired from, and Loraine rarely supported anything Kelly did.

She most definitely would not support Kelly being here, in Oyster Bay.

"Wouldn't it be nice to get paid for doing something that you love?" Evie said, as if reading her thoughts. Evie had a knack for doing that. No wonder her career was on the fast track.

"It would be," Kelly said slowly. She chewed her bottom lip as she imagined the things she would make. Hats and gloves and scarves were a dime a dozen. But for a Christmas Bazaar, she would make stockings, just like the ones she had made for herself, Evie, and Hannah. Beautiful, one of a kind, heirloom stockings. Stockings that would be pulled out of storage each December with a smile, and then hung above a roaring fire, an annual fixture.

Hannah sipped her drink and smiled her appreciation. "You can make them while we're at work this week."

Suddenly all of her good feelings vanished. "You have to work this week?" Kelly couldn't keep the disappointment from creeping into her tone, even though she wished she could. Of course her sisters had to work. The paper went out daily and they were on staff. Unlike her, they had things to do, responsibilities and all that.

"We'll be off next weekend so long as we have everything in by Friday, and Liam is letting us all work from home Christmas week," Hannah promised her.

"Except he'll be in there every day and night, I'm sure," Evie said with a sigh. She glanced across the room at the handsome man who ran the paper and back at them, her smile a little wistful.

Kelly couldn't help it. Her mind went to a dark place. Images of Brian and Shannon laughing on their way out of the gym, smoothies in hand, fornication no doubt minutes away.

"You okay?" Evie asked.

"Just thirsty," Kelly said, thinking that some punch might be nice. She walked to the dessert table, past faces she didn't recognize, wondering if she stared at them long enough if she'd be able to guess who they were, and knowing that she probably would. Oyster Bay had been a fantasy, another world, a place of characters and stories and myths and secrets.

Everyone here felt like a mild celebrity. Someone she had known from afar. Untouchable.

She studied the plates of cookies in all different shapes and flavors, hoping she didn't end up standing in the corner grazing all night, or worse, clinging to her sisters, who clearly knew everyone else here and were now busy doing the rounds, Evie at Liam's side, and Hannah with Dan. Now Evie was waving to her, so was Liam, and really, she should stop thinking about the cookies and go over to meet the man who had made ever practical Evie believe in romance and love and all that mushy stuff, but damn it if it didn't make her think about Brian. And she hated thinking about Brian.

Brian who was probably shagging Shannon at this very moment. Or about to, once Sunday yoga class was over. He never missed it. And now, well, she'd had to miss it. Every week.

She picked up a piece of fudge, the biggest one on the tray, and crammed it into her mouth. That was better.

"Kelly?" She turned at the sound of her voice to see a girl about her age, with Margo's coloring, and gleaming green eyes who could be no one else but…

She covered her mouth with her hand, imagining the chocolate coating her teeth. "Abby?"

"Did someone say Kelly?" An older woman with sharp eyes but a kind smile walked over to them, double fisting eggnog, which she was quick to explain. "One is for my husband, Earl. He's the one over near the piano, snoring. These dark days do it to him every time."

Kelly swallowed the fudge quickly, noticing the man in the bow tie on the oversized chairs, whose head seemed to jerk every few moments before he dozed off again.

"This is my grandmother," Abby explained. "Mimi, you know Kelly is Hannah and Evie's sister—"

"Oh, I know," Mimi said. "Everyone knows about Kelly, of course."

Did they? And what did they think? That she was the love child of Loraine and her father? That she was an inadvertent home-wrecker? That she had taken a mother away from two young girls, left them alone with—

Well, she thought. There was no easy way to finish that sentence. After all, they'd grown up with an adoring father, a doting aunt, three fun-loving cousins who were happy to share their grandmother.

Would Mimi bring her in the way she had Hannah and Evie? After all, Mimi was no relationship to them either.

"And how's your mother?" Mimi asked, as the air seemed to come out of the room.

Kelly's eyes darted nervously. Really, what was there to say? That her mother was having an affair with her yoga instructor, something Kelly had only learned after inadvertently stumbling upon them spoon feeding each other rice pudding in a restaurant that was now banned from her life, much like the gym now was, thanks to Brian's equally nefarious behavior?

"Has she changed her ways?" Mimi asked. She stood firmly, patiently waiting for a response, and Kelly finally gave in.

"No." After all, lying would have only complicated things, and she had no facts to back it up. Loraine was a lost soul, at least that was how she'd learned to rationalize it over the years. Someone who still didn't know who she was or what she wanted. Someone who would never be satisfied, at least, that's what her therapist said. Kelly had never been comforted by that thought, though.

Mimi barked out a laugh. "I had a feeling I would like you," she said, patting Kelly's arm.

Kelly felt like she might sink to the ground, so great was her relief as Mimi went off to deliver the eggnog to her husband.

Abby shook her head. "She's lost her filter."

Kelly finally poured herself some punch and drank it back, quickly. "I figured my presence here would be a little controversial."

"No more controversial than the rest of us," Abby said. She looked across the room, where Mimi was now talking to Sarah and a woman Kelly hadn't noticed earlier. "Oh, dear. She's probably giving out dating advice again."

"Dating advice?" Not that she was interested, per se, but well, she sort of needed all the help she could get.

Abby gave her a fearful look. "Trust me, you don't want to hear it. Unless adding a bit more lipstick or batting your eyelashes sound like useful tips?"

Kelly laughed. "Hey, it worked for her."

"I should save them." Abby sighed, refilling her glass of punch. "If I'm not back in five, will you save me?"

"Deal."

In her back pocket, her phone started to vibrate, and she had that momentary thought that it might be Brian, a jerk reaction she was hoping that her twice weekly therapy sessions with Dr. Chandler would have broken by now. She glanced down at the screen, hoping that her sisters didn't see the name that flashed across it, but they were talking about the Christmas Bazaar now, and so Kelly slipped into the hallway, and then, to be safe, out the front door.

"Hey, Loraine," she said, ducking out onto the front porch. The wind was fierce and she didn't have a coat, but the pounding of her heart kept her all too warm.

"I thought you should know that Chaz and I broke up," her mother said crisply.

"Oh." Kelly frowned. It wasn't exactly the most normal thing to do, to call your daughter and tell her that your affair was over, but then, nothing about their family dynamic had ever been something that Kelly would classify as traditional.

She struggled for words. "I'm sorry" didn't seem right, considering her father was still a part of this scenario. And "That's great news" seemed a bit callous, though not really.

"I think you made the right decision," she said instead, and that much was the truth. Long ago she'd given up on that perfect family image she'd always longed for. Gone was the hope for a mother who made her hot tea and tucked her into bed when she was sick. Gone was the hope that she and her father and mother would sit around a dinner table and laugh and tell stories. Her father was a workaholic, and Loraine was…well, up until today, Loraine was sleeping with Chaz, who had a man bun.

Kelly closed her eyes, trying to ban the image of those spandex covered thighs from her mind. Chaz was gone, out of the picture and now…

"I want us to all have a proper family Christmas," Loraine announced.

Kelly's mouth went dry. She licked her lips, turned and looked through the frosted window at the party going on behind her. The Christmas tree was lit by what seemed like thousands of lights, and someone had taken a seat at the piano. Dan was dancing with Lucy and Jack was dancing with Emma, and Evie, noticing her through the window, was smiling at her.

Kelly smiled back and held up a finger, signaling that she'd be back in a minute.

Her heart was thumping and her mind was spinning, and for one horrible, fleeting moment she felt guilty. And she didn't want to feel guilty. These people in there, those two women, were her sisters. And she wanted to spend her holiday with them, for once, finally.

"Christmas has never really been your thing, Mom," she pointed out, and it was the truth. Christmas usually consisted of take-out Chinese or, if her dad was feeling restless, a few burgers out on the grill. There were presents, of course, all wrapped by the stores they were bought from, so none of the paper matched. There were no carols or midnight masses or snowmen or sledding or gingerbread houses or traditions.

And she wanted traditions, damn it. She wanted these traditions, the ones that Hannah and Evie had shared.

"You knew I made plans for the holiday," she reminded her mother. Of course, she hadn't told her the real plans, but still.

"And you can't change them for the sake of family?"

Loraine insisted. She sounded incredulous, and for some reason, maybe it was because it was all too little too late, Kelly felt angry.

"Last year we went out for sushi on Christmas. The Christmas before that you were at a spa in Arizona. We haven't had a real family Christmas in…" Never, she thought. Instead she managed to say, "A long time."

"Which is why this is the year to start!" Loraine lowered her voice, sounding almost repentant when she said, "I know I've made some mistakes, Kelly. I want to make some changes."

Kelly clenched a fist at her side. Loraine's changes usually involved going vegan, or hitting a health spa for a month, or, of course, taking up yoga…

"I want to make things up to you."

Now Kelly swallowed hard, fighting back the tears that stung the backs of her eyes, telling herself it was just the cold, the wind, that she wasn't used to it. But that wasn't all she wasn't used to. Her mother was reaching out, making an effort, and Kelly didn't quite know what to do about that.

All her life, her family had been divided in two. Her sisters on one coast, her parents on another. And now she had a decision to make. How was she going to spend this Christmas, after all?

*

Noah turned on the television and then immediately turned it off again. Of course, it was this time of year, when you couldn't turn on the television or radio or even walk into a store without hearing every family's favorite jingle, advertising Keepsake's sugar cookies.

Now he was forced to listen to NPR, which had its moments, but got old after a while, especially after a long day at the office, when all he wanted to do was get home and heat up a frozen pizza and pour a cold one, then collapse on the sofa in the den with Murphy at his side. And you couldn't walk into a single shop in town without seeing the Christmas tin (gold with red polka-dots) tied with a signature red bow that always sold out before the holiday arrived.

He hated the sight of those cookies. Hated the taste, too. But more than anything he hated the jingle, and he should know, because he wrote it.

He smiled to himself, amazed that he'd managed to keep that little secret to himself all these years later. Of course, everyone knew that the creator of the best sugar cookie recipe in New England was Sandra Branson, his grandmother. And when she'd passed away six years ago, they knew that he and his only cousin had taken over the company, oversaw the numbers and the employees and the paperwork. The baking took place in a factory ten miles north of town. The marketing department had grown to thirty over the years, and since Gran's death, profits had skyrocketed. What had once been a small-town business was now a national moneymaker, and Christmas was their biggest season.

His marketing department had big plans, hoping to capture the European market next year, but then, none of them knew about his talks with Jerry Dubrow at Dubrow Foods or the deal that was being negotiated behind the scenes. It had been his cousin Allie's idea, and it hadn't taken long to convince him that selling was the best option he had, only he suspected she hadn't wrestled with the idea for even ten minutes, that to her it was only business, whereas to him it was so much more.

She hadn't grown up with Gran, not the way that he had. She hadn't stood in the kitchen of the house he now lived in and helped stir the batter, then set each cookie on the baking sheet, carefully measured to exactly one small scoop size, and then waited with growing impatience for those cookies to come out of the oven, because Gran always let him have the first taste.

And she hadn't been the face of the company, at the tender age of four, wearing overalls and sporting a cowlick and biting into an oversized cookie, his blue eyes digitally enhanced for effect. Allie had been in Boston, happily tucked in a brownstone, in a house he'd never seen, happy to take the twenty-five percent of her inheritance and grow it with him, all from Massachusetts, where she would take no heat for ruining Gran's good name and charitable intentions.

Most folks in town had stopped associating his face with the brand, mercifully. It had been the running joke all through middle school and high school, when kids got cruel about stuff like that, almost as bad as the comments people made on his clothes, on his lunch, on his house. A tiny little cottage Gran had happily named White Pine Cottage in an effort to brighten up their circumstances. It had done little good.

But nothing beat the comments people made about his mother. Or Keepsake Cookies.

Well, soon enough this would all be over, he reminded himself as agitation took over. Come the new year, Keepsake Cookies would be sold off to a national food chain, and the cottage, and every memory it ever held, would soon be a thing of the past.

Chapter Five

Kelly had a purpose for the first time since she'd lost her job, and by Tuesday afternoon she had run out of yarn. She stood from the sofa, her fingers cramped and stiff, and looked at the pile of stockings she had knitted, each one unique.

The snow that had fallen last night had cleared, and the sun shone in the clear blue sky. It was a cheerful winter day, and with the down parka that Bridget had given her to wear, along with the boots that were so much warmer and water-resistant than her leather ones, she decided to brave a trip into town for supplies.

There wasn't a yarn shop, but Evie had told her that there was a craft store across the street from Angie's Café, and from the display in the window of a paper-made Christmas village, Kelly didn't need to read the sign to know that she'd found the right place.

The front of the room of Beads and Bobbles featured gift items, stationary, and wrapping paper that looked far too pretty to ever rip. Kelly moved quickly past it, deciding to return after the Bazaar when she had more free time for Christmas shopping, and walked to the back wall, where balls of yarn were stacked in wooden crates. The selection was slim, but not unworkable, and Kelly immediately found a crate of holiday colors in soft cotton and wool blends, which she loaded into her basket.

"Do you have any more skeins?" she asked the woman at the cashier. "I'm knitting some items for Christmas, so I'm looking for more of the traditional colors. Some blues and golds, too."

The woman gave a smile and held up a finger. "Let me check the back room."

She returned a moment later with a box of unpackaged yarn. "I haven't gotten around to pricing these yet. But considering how much you're buying, I'll cut you a discount, if that works?

"Thank you!" Kelly gushed, eagerly reaching for a lovely ivory wool with a strand of gold tinsel thread running through it.

"You making gifts?" The woman—her nametag said Beth—set down the box of yarn and pulled a pricing sheet from her pocket.

"Sort of," Kelly said.

"We offer an open knitting night each Wednesday

from six to nine," the woman said with a smile. "Drop in if you're free tomorrow evening. No need to make a reservation in advance. Some weeks we have two people, some weeks we have ten."

"I just might," Kelly said, thinking of how busy her sisters were this week. She hadn't considered that other people were still working the week before Christmas when she'd made her plans. A sure sign that she had been unemployed for far too long.

The familiar sense of panic bubbled up when she considered that her unemployment checks would soon stop. That no one had called her back for an interview. That she wasn't so sure how long she could continue to pay rent on her pricey San Francisco apartment, no matter how small it was. That moving back in with Loraine was always a possibility, and one she really didn't want to pursue.

"Are you a beginner or an advanced knitter?" Beth asked, as Kelly picked up a skein of red merino wool and added it to her basket.

Kelly didn't want to put on airs any more than she wanted to dumb down her skill set, especially if she planned to sell any of her goods at the Bazaar.

"I'm not sure," she said. She motioned to the cowl at her neck, one she was particularly proud of, given the complicated stitch she had mastered to finish it. "I made this recently."

Beth's eyes widened and then narrowed. "That makes you an expert then."

Kelly blushed. "Well, I wouldn't go that far, but I enjoy it."

"Did your mother teach you to knit?" Beth asked, and although Kelly knew she was just making conversation, she wished the phone would ring, or someone would step into the shop and interrupt this conversation.

Her mother hadn't taught her much, at least not directly. Things like pouring cereal for dinner and knowing when she should probably go to bed so that she wasn't too tired for school the next day, sure. But it wasn't like Loraine had ever made cookies with her, or even taught her how to ride a bike. Her dad had taught her, when she finally asked enough times, just like he had taught her to drive a car too. He was a good man, but a man who wasn't around very much either.

"No, it was sort of thing back when I was college," Kelly explained. "All the girls were knitting, it was a popular thing to do, and well, I've always liked to create things."

"Then you should definitely come to one of our knitting nights. You could be our guest of honor." Beth extended her hand, smiling warmly, and it was then that Kelly realized she was actually quite young, and pretty too. She might have only been a couple years older than her. "I'm Beth Sanders."

"Kelly Myers. Hannah and Evie Donovan's sister," she added, hesitantly, but only because in a town this small, she suspected it wasn't long before word got out, or the follow-up question about why she was in town and for how long was spoken. "From California."

Beth's eyes rounded. "Hannah was in my grade at school. I remember her talking about how she was going out to California to meet her mother and sister after graduation."

"Yep," Kelly said. "And she did."

"Well, you look a lot like her. I'm surprised I didn't put it together when you walked in. But then, we get a lot of tourists in Oyster Bay. Not many at Christmas, though." She placed a skein of purple yarn back with its couple group. "Staying at the inn, I suppose?"

She meant the Harper House Inn, no doubt, given its ties to the Donovans. Kelly shook her head. "No, renting a place for a few weeks."

The answer seemed to satisfy Beth, and for a moment, Kelly wanted to say exactly which place she was renting, see if it sparked the same reaction in this shop owner that it had in her sisters. But the door jingled a new arrival and the moment was lost as Beth turned to attend to a woman and a small child, offering an apologetic smile.

"Just let me know if you need anything," she said, setting a hand on Kelly's elbow, and Kelly turned back to the wall of yarn with a happy heart. This really was turning out to be the best Christmas ever.

And no amount of guilt that weighed on the back of her mind about her mother would take away from it.

She filled her basket, took a flyer for the open knitting night, and, after one more walk around the room to admire the offerings, walked to the counter. "Well, these are nice!" she said, gesturing to a display of Christmas tins, all tied with a thick velvet red bow. It was exactly the kind of gift she would have sent to her mother, if her mother was the kind of woman who ate cookies, or appreciated little gestures, or knew that she was in Oyster Bay, not on a ski trip with her girlfriends in Lake Tahoe.

"Local company," Beth said. "At least it was," she added, a strange undertone to her voice. "I'm surprised you've never seen these before. They're a pretty big company now."

Kelly didn't bother to explain that she'd grown up with a health food nut and that recently she'd taken to exclusively living off the junk from the frozen aisle.

She smiled at the old-fashioned photo of a little boy biting into a cookie that was the front of the label. "Keepsake Cookies. I'll take two," she said on a whim. She'd bring one back for her friend Lindsay, and the other she'd set out for dessert when her sisters came by, and she did hope they would stop by, and soon.

After all, who could resist cookies?

*

Noah used to love coming in town, especially as a kid. Back then, any escape from the cottage was a treat. School? He loved school, up until he didn't love it, that was. Then it turned to music, the guitar he had inherited from the father he'd never known, that he'd learned to play just by fooling around with the strings, mimicking songs from the radio, later, learning to read music from school, and Mr. Zimmerman, head of the music department, a good man through and through.

Sometimes, Noah wondered if Mr. Zimmerman was his father, given the connection they both had for music, and he'd finally worked up the courage to ask his mother, who looked up from the television long enough to burst out laughing, and she laughed and she laughed as he ran to his room and slammed the door and buried his head in the pillow, hating the tears that were wetting his cheeks. Hating that he even cared.

That was the last time he'd played the guitar. Well, the second to last time, he thought, thinking of the damn cookie jingle.

His mother, Gran had always said, had "problems." At first, he was too young to understand. She rarely came into town. She said she didn't like the way people looked at her. Said they judged her. That she was the black sheep in the royal family. Noah wondered when he was little if that meant he was a prince, but later he learned the Bransons were an old name in town, a wealthy family with a reputation. His grandfather was on the board of the school, the library, the planning committee. He was a professional philanthropist. Their house had been passed down through the generations. And their youngest child and only daughter, Noah's mother, was a grave disappointment.

There were fights at times, whenever they got together,

which was only at Christmas, and sometimes at Thanksgiving. Fights when Gran wouldn't bring out the wine, and Noah's mother asked why, and Gran's face would become pale and she'd look at Gramps, who'd give a weary sigh, and then tell Noah to get out of the room before the yelling started. He'd climb under the tree, stare up at the lights and escape, or he'd go up to the bedrooms, his mother's old room, look at the toys, which were still all in place, and stare out the big windows framed with lace curtains onto the small house at the bottom of the hill, wishing he didn't have to go back there.

Gran took Noah into town as often as she could, and she always wore her highest heels. In winter, she had a bright red coat with fur at the collar, and she had a special coat that she made him wear on those occasions, too. Noah's mother called her "shallow" for buying him these expensive items, but Noah didn't mind. He liked wearing the soft wool coat, and he liked sitting in the window of Carmine's, sipping a root beer float while Gran chatted with ladies who passed by, patted him on the head, and declared his grandmother to be the best baker in all of New England. She'd been winning every baking contest for years and, by demand, had been selling her cookies in town since around the time he was born.

Noah's mother had a brother, who *was* the prince, or so she said, but he was older, and lived in Boston with his wife and daughter. He'd made something of himself, his mother used to say, a little bitterly, and Noah decided that he liked the sound of that. That if making something of yourself meant living in Boston, instead of this cramped cottage at the bottom of the hill belonging to his grandparents, that he wanted to do just that.

And he had, he thought sadly, looking at the corner of Main and Fourth Street, where Carmine's used to be. Now, it was a bank. A business. Nothing personal about it. If he stared long enough, he could almost see Gran sitting in the window, her leather gloves set neatly on the counter, a large Coke float in front of her. "I always did have a sweet tooth," she'd sigh, and Noah would stare at her in wonder, because adults didn't drink kid drinks, did they? His mother drank "adult" beverages.

Now Noah hurried to his truck, the errands he'd needed to run finished. He was rarely out at this time of day, but the vet was closing early and as the owner of the company he had the flexibility to work from home this afternoon, even if he'd rather be in his office, ten miles away, shut behind a closed door. Town was something he now viewed through his mother's eyes, a place where people gathered, where he didn't belong, where people stared and speculated and said things that were none of their business.

Now he understood how his mother must have felt.

"Noah?"

He stopped, surprised at the sound of his name, something he didn't hear outside the workplace these days, and even then it was usually "Mr. Branson" or sometimes, more casually, "Sir."

Kelly was standing about twenty feet away, holding two shopping bags, wearing a yarn hat that was bright red, bringing out the rosiness in her cheeks.

"Kelly." He felt stiff, on edge, wondering if something was wrong with the cottage, if she needed something from him. Something he wouldn't be able to deliver.

He let people down, that's what he did. He let his mother down. He let the town down. And to hear people talk, he'd let Gran down, the one person he'd never wanted to hurt.

And now, now he was about to let down every single person who relied on him.

It was business, he told himself. That's what Allie had insisted. No different than the bank buying out the spot that used to hold Carmine's. No different than those memories being replaced with functionality.

"I fixed the shutter on the front window," Kelly informed him.

Noah had to admit, his pride stung at that one. "I would have gotten to it eventually," he said. Since he'd decided to start renting out the cottage a few years back, he'd had very few tenants, especially in the winter. Real estate was prime, but most tourists preferred a beach-front property, not a small house in the woods with less than ample natural light. Still, the few he had were quiet and kept to themselves.

None had been such a pain in the butt as Kelly. And

none had been as pretty either.

Not that he cared. Relationships weren't his thing. How could they be?

"You mean before you tore it down?" Kelly raised an eyebrow, and he knew she had him there.

"I mean, I can fix it. I could have. If you'd asked."

"A simple thank you will suffice," Kelly remarked. Her smile seemed prim, but there was no sense of gloating in her eyes.

Noah leveled her with a stare, but finally caved. "Thank you," he said, even though he didn't care, not at all. He didn't care that the cottage was falling apart; in a way it made it easier, didn't it?

"I thanked myself as well," Kelly added happily, and Noah looked at her strangely.

"Thanked yourself?"

"Don't you ever do that?" She shrugged. "You have to thank yourself once in a while, just like you have to pat yourself on the back, too. You can't rely on other people to do that for you in life." When she realized he was staring at her, her cheeks turned pink, and not from the wind. "Sorry. Years of therapy takes its toll."

Therapy, huh? So this overly chipper, optimistic tourist had some demons? He suddenly found her much more interesting.

"Anyway," she said, drawing a pattern in the snow with the tip of her boot, "Now I imagine I'll sleep better without that shutter banging in the wind all night long."

He shoved his hands in his pocket, feeling ashamed.

She was a guest, a paying one at that, and she deserved a decent place to stay while she was in town. "If I'd had more notice I would have—"

She held up a hand. "It's fine. I love it, actually."

Love it? How could anyone love that cottage? That place was cramped and dark and every time he walked in the door he felt tense. It was downright haunted, that's what it was.

And that was precisely why he didn't like it to stay empty, and why it needed to come down once and for all.

"So, you're really tearing it down?" she asked.

"Yep," he said, opening his door and setting the pharmacy bag of vet meds on the seat. Each time he picked up the prescription, he felt a wave of sadness. Murphy was getting on in years. Time was moving forward and change was ahead. And what was next? That was the part he hadn't figured out yet.

"Well, how much is the rent?" she asked, walking over to hover at the edge of the sidewalk.

"It's not for rent," he said firmly. If he'd spent a few bucks cleaning up the place, he could get a pretty penny for it, despite its location. Oyster Bay was full of summer people looking for a country getaway with access to the Atlantic. "It's being torn down once the ground has thawed."

"Why?" she asked.

He shrugged. He wasn't about to explain his reasons. "It's too much work. Besides, I have no use for it." And he didn't, not unless you counted being haunted by the past as a positive pastime.

"You could fix it up," she offered. "Paint the door, add a wreath, give the inside a little makeover with some fresh neutral colors and some cozy throws and pillows. With a little TLC, it could bring in more guests. Bridget told me how much these rentals go for at peak season."

Bridget Harper, no doubt. He recalled her being in real estate a while back. Now, she ran an inn. He wondered for a moment why Kelly hadn't stayed there, with her ties to the family, but refrained from asking. It would just prolong the conversation and really, it wasn't his business.

And more people in this town should learn to mind their business.

"I don't need the money," he said matter-of-factly.

She looked crestfallen, and he knew the debate was over. He set one foot in the truck, and then, because he was actually curious, for reasons he couldn't explain, even to himself, he turned and asked, "Why do you care so much?"

"Oh." She blew out a breath, and seemed to think about it for a moment. "I guess it's because it's where I'm spending my first Christmas here in this town. I've always wanted to come here and now I have. All my life I had to hear about the memories my sisters were making in Oyster Bay, and now it's my turn to have a few of my own. If the cottage is torn down, then it's like there won't be any physical reminder of my time here, and no chance to relive any of it either. Silly, I know." She looked down, turned to go.

"It's not silly," he said, his voice gruff. She'd captured his sentiments exactly.

She looked up at him, hopefully, "But not enough to make you change your mind?"

He considered it for a few, fleeting seconds, but longer than he had ever thought he would. That cottage was filled with memories. But unlike hers, his memories weren't all warm and fuzzy.

"The cottage is being torn down," he said. When it was gone, there would be no more looking back.

"Well, it was worth a try," she said a little sadly. She motioned to the packages on his seat. "Christmas shopping?"

He scoffed. "God, no." He didn't have anyone to buy anything for. Gran was long gone now, and he hadn't dated in a while. He had no siblings, and his parents…Well. This was why he hated Christmas, he thought. He was the outsider, looking in, seeing everything the way it should be and never was. And he hated self-pity. Refused to feed into it. Eleven months out of the year, he was fine doing his thing, not thinking about the fact that other people had it different, or better. But the holiday season had a way of stirring things up, reminding him that he wasn't just the little boy on the face of Keepsake Cookies. That the image was nothing like reality at all.

And it still wasn't, he thought, thinking of his

reputation around town.

Her eyes narrowed. "You say that as if you don't believe in Christmas."

"You're a sharp observer," he said with a grin.

"You mean to tell me that you live here, in this picture-perfect town, and that you truly do not feel the Christmas spirit in the air, all around you?"

He looked passively up and down Main Street. Twinkling lights and wreaths did little for him. What he saw was the same small town and the same narrow opportunities that had been here twenty years ago. "Nope."

"Interesting." She was looking him up and down, chewing her bottom lip. He didn't like the look in her eyes. It was like she knew something that he didn't. "I have an offer for you."

"An offer?"

"On the cottage," she said brightly.

He stifled a sigh. "I told you. It's not for sale."

"I know it's not for sale. And I know that money doesn't matter to you. You made that very clear." She took a step toward him, and in the clear, cold, winter light, her dark eyes were a sharp contrast to pale skin and rosy cheeks. She was certainly pretty, in a natural sort of way. She probably didn't even know she was pretty, and she certainly didn't work hard at it. She wore no makeup, and her hair was in a loose ponytail under one of those ridiculous hats she was always wearing, it seemed.

"I have a deal for you, Mr. Branson," she said cheekily.

Despite his better judgment, he couldn't help but be intrigued. Most people in town barely spoke to him, and here was this woman, fresh faced and eager, all too happy to wear him down and, dare he say, befriend him.

It would only be a matter of time before someone tipped her off. Scared her straight about Gran's no-good grandson who had sold out against her wishes. "She's crying in her grave," Dottie Joyce, head of the historical society and professional busybody, had clucked when he bumped into her at the grocery store a few months after he'd taken over the business. Since then he started having the groceries delivered, or he stopped at a bigger store, outside town, on his way back from the office space he'd rented to house the growing corporation.

"A deal?"

"That's right. A deal. If I can make you a believer in the magic of Christmas by December 25, then you don't tear down the cottage."

He hadn't seen that coming, and he didn't even bother to turn her down. "Okay, Miss Myers," he said. "You have a deal."

Her eyes shot open and she whooped with delight. He felt bad about that, but something about her joy, her radiant happiness was almost, well, contagious.

He took a step backward, eager to get into his truck. Time to get back to real life again. Kelly, after all, was just a temporary distraction. A sweet woman who was passing through town with the best of intentions. She didn't know the half of it.

"You wait and see, Noah. I'll make you a believer before Christmas if it's the last thing I do!" she called after him.

He shook his head as he climbed up onto the driver's seat. She wouldn't. No one could. And come the spring, that cottage, and every memory it had ever held, would be gone for good.

*

Kelly thought of her plan the entire walk home. Home. It was a funny word for a rundown cottage with a creaky front stoop and an unreliable furnace, but as it appeared in the distance, at the end of the plowed path, nestled in a bed of tall, snow-frocked pine trees, she realized that that was what it was: home.

And she wasn't about to let it go.

After all, what did she have waiting for her back home in California? Brian was gone. He wasn't coming to his senses about Shannon, and thanks to many emails with Evie, she realized that she didn't want him back anyway. He was no good, down and dirty, and she should have seen that from the beginning, before she'd started to care. But she had cared. Enough to fall into a slump. Enough to lose her job. It wouldn't be long before she lost her apartment, too. For some reason, it didn't quite matter. Back in San Francisco she had friends, like Lindsay, but Lindsay still worked for the real estate firm and so gone were their lunch breaks and chats in the break room. And then there were her parents, of course.

Kelly swallowed the lump in her throat that rose every time she thought of that call with her mother. Two days had passed and she hadn't called her back. Loraine had left a text just this morning, with a picture of some Christmas ornaments she'd bought at Bloomingdales. Were these shiny new ornaments supposed to make up for the lack of homemade ones they had laying around the house? Christmas was supposed to be sentimental. There was nothing right about a store-bought Christmas.

She'd hung some greenery over the door that she'd bought in the town square from a stand selling Christmas trees. She intended to go back first chance she had for the tree itself, hopefully with Evie and Hannah this weekend, and she already had her eye on two good ones, nice and symmetrical and a good height, not too tall or too wide. She'd decorate it with the lights and garland she had in her suitcase stowed in the second bedroom, now quickly turning into her Christmas workshop.

She set the bags of yarn on the floor near the couch and the tins of cookies on the counter, grinning as a sudden idea took hold. Thanks to her little trip to the Corner Market the other night, she had all the ingredients she needed to make up a batch of cookies, and really, who *could* resist a Christmas cookie?

An hour later, she mustered up the courage to begin the trek up to the big house, not exactly sure what she would discover when she got there. The driveway was split at the base, and rather than walk all the way to the street, she took a path that hugged the tree line, where the snow was patchy and thin and she didn't have to worry about slipping and dropping the cookies, that smelled nearly as wonderful as the fresh pine. It was so dark she could barely carve her way, and only one light shone from within the back of the large house. Hardly welcoming.

Up close, the house was large, stately, and well maintained. Boxwoods flanked the door and hugged the lower level windows, and somewhere through one, she thought she saw the glow of a lamp.

Was he alone? Was he even home? She'd already decided to leave the cookies on the doormat, with a note, if he wasn't.

She studied the front door, black and a little foreboding, with one large, brass knocker, and a doorbell just to the side of the freshly painted frame. Well, one thing was for certain, this house was far better maintained than the more modest part of the property.

She pressed the bell, her heart speeding up as her finger released from the button and chimes could be heard, followed by the barking of a dog.

A light in the hallway came on and a little brown face appeared through the window that framed the door, and she rose her eyes to see Noah standing behind the dog, glowering at her.

"What's going on? Is there a problem?" His eyes darted past her, in the direction of the cottage.

Curious. Was he actually concerned about the cottage?

Maybe it was just concern to have to deal with it, she corrected herself.

Forcing a smile against his grumpiness, she held her plate of cookies a little higher. "I brought you some cookies."

His lip seemed to curl as his eyes drifted to the plate of, admittedly, the world's not so prettiest cut-out cookies.

"They lost their shape a bit in the oven," she admitted. "But I added plenty of sprinkles to cover up the mistakes."

"No thank you," he said.

Kelly blinked at him. Was he actually...*rejecting* her not so perfect homemade cookies? "They taste better than they look." And they did. She'd had three herself, when she remembered she had been so busy knitting she had forgotten to eat lunch, something that often happened when she picked up a fresh ball of yarn.

"I don't like cookies," he said bluntly.

She stared at him, not knowing how to even respond to that, and then felt her anger subside when she looked down at the furry little guy standing close to Noah's knee, a hopeful look in his warm brown eyes, and a tail that was just begging for some attention.

"Well, hello there," she said, thrusting the plate at Noah as she bent to stroke the dog's head.

Noah muttered something in exasperation, but she refused to acknowledge him, not when this cutie was now licking her face and snuggling a little closer.

"He's adorable," Kelly said, looking up at the less than pleased Noah. "What's his name?"

"Murphy," Noah said with overt reluctance.

"Murphy." Kelly closed her eyes and nuzzled the dog's face. "Do you like cookies, Murphy? I bet you do. Yes, I bet you do."

"He's on a special diet," Noah said firmly.

Kelly pursed her lips, stifling a sigh at the hard shell she was unable to crack. Yet. "I always wanted a dog," she said, pushing herself up to a standing position. When Noah just stared at her blankly, she said, "How long have you had him?"

"Thirteen years," Noah said, and then, something in his eyes shifted. "But he's a mutt and his lifespan is long."

And there it was, Kelly thought. The man did, in fact, have a heart. "Well, he seems healthy as a young pup," she assured him, and again something shifted in his eyes. Relief, perhaps.

"I need to take him for a walk now," Noah said, excusing her. He tried to push the cookies toward her hands but she backed away quickly.

"Take them to work if you don't want them. Spread a little holiday cheer!"

He looked bewildered, staring at the plate as if he didn't quite know how to react to that. "But—"

"Murphy's waiting for his walk!" she said merrily. She backed away, out of reach, feeling a little victorious.

She'd managed to take him out of his comfort zone,

she thought with a grin as she turned back toward the cottage. She'd call that progress. And even though she hadn't managed to thaw his heart through his stomach, thanks to Murphy, there might just be another way…

Chapter Six

Noah pushed through the doors of Keepsake Cookies at seven sharp the next morning, eager to get to his desk before any of his staff rolled in. They made him uneasy, at least recently, with hints of annual bonuses and their big holiday plans. Maybe it was the guilt of knowing half of them would probably lose their jobs in the buy-out. Or maybe it was just the season. But so long as he could keep the door to his office shut until the first week of January, then that worked for him.

He walked past the small Christmas tree his assistant, Meryl, a forty-ish woman with a penchant for bright clothing, kept on her desk, the edge of his coat accidentally sending it askew as he brushed past. Annoyed, he straightened it, even forced himself to adjust some of the colored lights that had been messed up by the near fall, and then forcefully opened his door and closed it. No more trees. No more music. No more, God willing, talk of the annual Christmas cookie, which now changed each year. This year's flavor was eggnog. Not original, but when it came to Christmas, he'd learned that people preferred tradition, and anything that broke code was offensive. Or at least, so Allie had insisted when she sensed his hesitation about the bell shape she gave the stamp of approval to back in July.

Even in the summer, they were talking about Christmas. There was no getting away from it. It was a money maker. And Christmas and cookies went together like, well, cookies and milk, or so their holiday jingle said.

The jingle was banned from the office. He'd made sure of that right from the start. When his vice-president, a middle-aged woman with three teenage sons and a gift for keeping her opinions to herself, lifted an eyebrow, he said that he felt classical music set a more professional mood for the lobby.

His office was on the top floor, with a view of the factory that was located on the western edge of the property. He closed the door behind him, happy to close out all the Christmas decorations, too. He kept his office the same, three hundred sixty-five days a year. In the entire six years since he had inherited Gran's carefully guarded secret cookie recipes and, with Allie's share and input, turned a small, local business into a privately owned company, he had never once taken a vacation day.

How could he?

These cookies, this company, were Gran's legacy. And, according to local legend, he had bastardized it.

All the more reason to be done with it, he thought, dropping his coat onto a hook on the back of the door and walking around his desk to his leather rolling chair. There was an email from Allie waiting for him, subject line, "Dubrow."

His heart sped up at the name, at all it meant, and implied. It meant game over. That he'd given up. Been beaten down. That they won. And wasn't that the one thing he'd promised himself never to do, all those years ago, when he'd stood at his mother's grave? He'd sworn then that it would all be different for him.

But it wasn't different at all. In fact, it was eerily the same.

He bypassed the email and picked up the phone, speed dialing Allie with the press of a button. She'd be at her satellite office in Boston by now. Like him, she was not married and had no domestic responsibilities outside of a Pomeranian named Sugar, but the similarities ended there.

"What's up?" she answered in her usual crisp, impatient way. He could hear her tapping, and it was evident he was on speaker, not that there was anyone to overhear their conversation. When they'd started the company, Allie preferred to keep her Boston address, and they'd worked out a system where she drove in a few times a month for important meetings, handling everything else remotely.

The business ran smoothly with the setup. The only thing that wasn't so simple was the talk around town. Something that Allie had been able to dodge, considering no one in Oyster Bay knew her.

"I saw your email." He skimmed it quickly, frowning at what he saw. "You want to move the meeting to next Friday?"

"Do you have a problem with that?" More tapping at the keyboard. The bulk of Allie's responsibilities lay in marketing, while his was in operations. Now he wondered how much of her time was being spent on the buy-out instead.

All of it, he presumed. Another differentiation between their roles was that he had to put on a game face around the office. Allie was known to throw a work shirt over her pajamas on video conference calls.

"Will we be ready in time?" Their lawyers had been meeting for weeks, finalizing the details, but something was still holding Noah back, a sense of unfinished business, something that had been overlooked.

"We'll make ourselves ready," Allie said. "Besides, I want to get away for the holiday, and I'd love to have this wrapped up by then. Jerry will come to our office. I'll drive in next Friday morning."

And out later that night, no doubt. He and Allie had never been close. As children, Allie's family had rarely visited Oyster Bay and his mother had bitter feelings about her only sibling, and it shone through on those get togethers. Gran had pushed him into going to college in Boston, but he'd preferred New York, a place he could get lost in the crowd, where no one knew him unless he wanted them to.

He could go back, he considered... But the thought of it wasn't as appealing as he wished it to be.

"So next Friday. Ten? That will give us time to gather our thoughts privately beforehand." The typing stopped and suddenly Allie's voice became loud and clear on the other end of the receiver. "You don't have anything else going on that day, do you?"

Noah checked his calendar. Next Friday was Christmas Eve. "Nope. Nothing at all."

"Good. I know Jerry's just as eager to wrap this up as we are. I'll see you next Friday morning for the final meeting." And with that, she disconnected the call.

The final meeting, where, with any luck, an agreement would be finalized, terms would be met, hands would be shaken, and Noah could walk out the door knowing that he was nearly a free man. That before long, this company, and all that it had represented and become, would no longer be his responsibility. That Keepsake Cookies would live on, as he knew Gran would have wanted it to, but that he would no longer be the face of the company. Or the scapegoat.

And when he put it that way, he could hardly wait.

*

What Kelly needed to do, she decided as she walked into town, was look at her list. Her list of all the activities that would lead to a perfect Christmas might not be what her sisters had in mind, but it just might help her get Noah Branson get into the holiday spirit. Item number one was already scratched: homemade Christmas cookies. Next on the list was homemade gifts, and she had just the idea for that one.

She checked her watch, deciding that she had just enough time to stop by the post office and mail her tin of cookies before the knitting group started. When she'd texted her sisters about it this morning, Hannah made her apologies but Evie accepted, something that both excited and worried Kelly. Alone with Evie, with no Hannah as buffer? But then, would it really be so different than the emails, texts, and phone calls they had shared these last couple of months?

It would be good to bond. And at least she'd have a pair of knitting needles in her hands to help her stay calm.

She scanned the post office for boxes, but seeing only padded envelopes and crate-size cardboard options, she approached the desk. A kind-looking woman with sharp blue eyes that nearly matched her hair greeted her with a smile.

"I was hoping to mail this, but I don't see any boxes," Kelly said.

The woman looked fondly at the tin of cookies and

then clucked her tongue. "That little Noah Branson was such a handsome child. Shame he's turned into such an Ebenezer."

Kelly frowned. How did this woman know she knew Noah? And what was this about Ebenezer?

"He's miserly, that one. Sandy Branson was my best friend," the woman confided. She leaned over the counter separating them, her eyes squinting at the memory. "Didn't care a thing about money, even though she'd grown up with a silver spoon, of course, big house on the hill, one of the founding families of Oyster Bay. Her father was the mayor when we were little, and she used to invite me over for tea. They were very proper like that. Sandy always wore a nice dress when she came into town, from the time she was in pigtails right up until the day she died. But she wasn't a snob. She'd invite me over for tea and then, afterward, we'd slip into the kitchen and help the cook. That's where she learned to bake. Started this company right out of her own kitchen." She tapped the tin for good measure.

"You mean…" Kelly tried to follow the information coming at her. "That your friend—Noah's grandmother started this company?"

The woman (her name tag said Kitty) nodded. "That's right. Everyone loved those sugar cookies, and Sandy loved making them. They were limited batches, and she'd give them away for free if they made people happy, and a lot of times she did, especially at the Christmas Eve tree lighting, and everyone looked forward to it, too. She put her heart into every single cookie she made. Those tins were her idea. Said she wanted her cookies to be just as nice on the outside as they were on the inside. Said she wanted each one to feel like a gift."

Kelly looked down at the picture of the little boy and almost gasped as it all came together. Those eyes. They were so blue. No one had eyes like that. Except…She tapped the tin. "Noah. *This* is Noah?" She stared at the picture, trying to imagine the grumpy landlord as this sweet little boy.

"Apple of her eye, that's what he was, especially after what a disappointment her daughter turned out to be. Died with a broken heart, poor Sandy." Kitty clucked again and pinched her lips together. "I'm just happy she didn't live to see what her beloved Noah has gone and done."

Kelly swallowed hard, feeling a chill run down her spine at such an ominous declaration. "So who runs Keepsake Cookies now?"

"Well, Noah, of course. Took his share and his cousin Allie's and ruined all of their grandmother's good intentions. Took her heart and soul and turned it into a cash machine, made it everything she didn't want it to become. Pinched every penny and laid off every hard worker here in town who knew Sandy's recipes by heart, and only after serving them with some legal papers saying they would sue if those recipes were ever shared, mind you. Noah moved all the baking to a factory about ten miles from here. Mass production." She looked around as another person walked in, and clearly deciding they could wait, leaned forward and said, "He's a greedy boy. Takes after his mother. No heart. Cold as ice."

"And the cousin?"

"Oh, well…she's the daughter of Sandra's son, Leo. Leo is a very successful banker in Boston. She's more of a silent partner, no doubt. She's never been seen around town, not since the grandparents both died. No, this is all Noah's doing."

Kelly blinked, not quite sure just how to respond to that one, but luckily, she didn't have to. All at once, Kitty decided she had vented enough and she stood straighter, patted her thinning blue-tinted hair and put on her reading glasses. "Now, let's get this label taped up. Where'd you say you were sending this?"

By the time Kelly left the post office, her bag only slighter lighter, her tread felt a hundred times heavier. Everyone in this town was warning her against Noah, and everyone in this town seemed to think he was someone, well, terrible.

She thought back to way he'd looked at Murphy, the sadness in his eyes when the dog's age came up.

All the more reason to stick to her plan. She'd save the cottage by Christmas. And maybe, just maybe, she'd save Noah, too.

*

Beads and Bobbles was all lit up when Kelly pushed

through the door a few minutes later, and she was surprised to see that at least three other people were already gathered at the old farm table at the back of the room, their fingers already hard at work, clicking wooden needles, some preferring the metal variety.

She didn't need to investigate long to determine that Evie had not yet arrived. A part of her worried that maybe Evie wouldn't come at all, that maybe she got busy with something, something with Liam, or Hannah, or her father, who ran a seafood restaurant at the edge of town and where she sometimes helped out on busy nights.

For a long time, when Hannah would describe the food her father served there (lobster bisque, seafood gumbo, crab cakes, double stuffed potatoes) Kelly could imagine eating there first thing if she ever finally made it to Oyster Bay. But that was when she was still young, still a little naïve, not fully aware of the circumstances that led to Loraine divorcing Chip, leaving him with two young daughters, never to return again.

"Oh, good, you came!" Beth said brightly, motioning to the table. "Feel free to take any seat you'd like."

"I'm waiting for someone," Kelly explained, just to be sure she snagged two adjacent chairs.

"A friend?" A burly man with kind eyes who was working on a rather impressive sweater smiled at her.

Kelly licked her bottom lip and said, "My sister."

"Don't think I've ever seen you in here before," the man said as he quickly knitted another row of a sleeve.

He was using circular needles, and by the ease of his movement, it was clear he had done this before.

"I'm visiting from California," she replied, and then, because she couldn't help herself, she said, "You're really good at this."

"Keeps me out of trouble," the man said with a wink, and Kelly laughed, because she could probably say the same. After all, when she was first unemployed, and heartbroken over Brian, she'd kept her hands busy in the chips bag, or clicking the television remote. Now, thanks to the knitting, she had a purpose. And thanks to the Christmas Bazaar, she had a job of sorts.

She set her handbag on the chair she was saving for Evie and then removed her newest stocking from a plastic bag, along with her needles and a skein of yarn. She had brought enough to finish the project and start another, just in case she and Evie decided to stay for the full three hours. Now, being here with others who shared her interest, she decided she wouldn't mind doing just that.

She thought about her deal with Noah and set her stocking to the side. She would finish that once the other project was complete.

The table fell into companionable silence, and Kelly cast on a row, following the pattern she'd studied on her phone earlier today. It was simple, really, and while the cotton yarn wasn't her favorite to work with (she'd prefer a delicate cashmere or a frothy angora), she was particularly excited about this project.

When the bells above the door jangled, she'd nearly forgotten her sister was supposed to be meeting her at all, until she looked up and saw her smiling face as she reached to pull off her hat. Store-bought, of course. Though Evie was keen to tell her patients (and sister) to knit away their troubles, she didn't follow her own advice.

"Evie!" the man knitting the sweater cried out. His entire face beamed as bright as the star atop a Christmas tree.

"I had a feeling I'd see you here," Evie said, coming around the table. She dropped onto the seat as Kelly moved her handbag, leaving Kelly at the head of the table, with her sister and the sole man in the room on either side of her.

Evie leaned forward and fingered the sweater the man was making, "Wow! When I told you to start knitting, I had no idea you would take me this seriously!"

The man gave a bashful grin. "Well, it does help me, and when I was just doing scarves it wasn't quite enough to keep my mind from wandering to places it's not supposed to."

"No more hacking Facebook accounts then?" Evie asked with a little smile.

The man seemed mildly disappointed as he worked the needles. "No."

"No more drive-bys or convenient run-ins at the dry cleaners?"

The man sighed. "No."

"I'm proud of you!" Evie looked genuinely pleased until the man glanced up from his sweater and gave her a strange look. Evie's smile fell. "What happened?"

The man's eyes darted around the room as he leaned across the table. Suddenly, almost just now remembering she was there, he said to Kelly, "It's okay if you hear about it. I've already decided you're cool."

"This is my sister," Evie told him, and just hearing those words made Kelly feel like it was Christmas morning then and there.

She smiled shyly at the man who frowned at her now, and then back at Evie. "That's right," she said. "Half-sister. From California."

She expected the man to comment on the weather, or some familial resemblance, even if it was to Hannah, but instead he looked at her earnestly and said, "You are a very, very lucky woman to be related to Evie. She is a gift. An absolute angel."

Evie rolled her eyes, but Kelly could tell she was flattered. "Enough stalling now. What happened?"

"Oh. That." The man shifted back to his project, refusing to make eye contact with Evie. "Well, you remember how I was having trouble hacking into her email account?"

Evie's mouth was set, her eyes firm. "Yes," she said flatly.

Kelly dropped a stitch. This was just getting too good!

"Well, I uh, finally got in." The man had to lick his lip to try to hide his smile, but oh, he did a very poor job of it. Kelly felt the giggles coming on and starting furiously biting her own lip, but it was no use. Evie, on the other hand, was far from amused.

"We discussed this." She eyed him steadily. Her expression was flat.

"I know," the man said, his shoulders slumping. "But I had to see…"

"See what?" Evie's voice was firm rather than curious, like Kelly, who had set her knitting on the table now because she was more eager to know just what this man discovered in someone else's email account.

"Look, she writes these emails to her best friend in New York. Every day. She was doing it as long as I've known her. They tell each other everything, and well, I was wondering if she ever mentioned me. If she, you know, missed me."

Kelly looked over at Evie, whose lips were pushed out in overt disappointment, but her eyes had softened a bit. "Jill has moved on with her life."

"I know." But he said it like a man who did not know.

"When people decide they want a change and do not want to continue a relationship, you can fight for it, but eventually, you have to accept the fact that if they are determined to go, they will go, and that it isn't always the other person's fault. Sometimes, no matter what you do, you can't make someone love you, you can't make them stay with you, and you can't keep holding on."

Kelly picked up her needles and focused on the project

in her hands. Was this how Evie felt about Loraine? She seemed so firm in her belief. Was it really so easy? Or was this just tough love?

"Has it helped you to sit outside Dave's house and stare in the windows, looking for Jill?" Evie asked, and the man shook his head. "Or breaking into her Facebook account and reinstating your marital status?"

Kelly must have gasped audibly at that one because both the man and Evie glanced at her. Quickly, she returned to her project.

Evie sighed. "You're a great guy with a lot to offer. You will get through this. And I'm glad you've joined something, that you're here, part of the community, doing something positive, just for you."

Something about all this sounded vaguely familiar. A man who was struggling to get over his wife, cheating on him...And the knitting. Of course! It all started to click. She leaned forward, whispering so no one else would hear. "Is your name *Don* by any chance?"

The man's cheeks turned a little red, but his grin was rueful. "Don is my pen name. My...alter ego. Don't need everyone knowing my business, after all."

"Of course not," Kelly agreed, nodding.

"My real name is Ron," he said, shifting his eyes around the table. "So let's just, uh, keep the whole Don thing between us."

Kelly bit down on her lip. Hard. "Of course," she promised, and glanced over to see Evie fluttering her lashes in exasperation. Still, it was clear she had a soft spot for Don—make that, Ron—if the little smile on her lips said anything.

"What are you making?" Ron asked, seeming eager to change the subject.

Now this Kelly was excited about. "It's a rope toy."

"For a dog?" Evie asked, seeming confused.

"A gift," Kelly said with a smile and went back to her work. She hoped that Murphy would like it. She hoped he would play with it every single day, and she hoped that Noah's heart would thaw, just a bit, and that maybe, just maybe her time at the cottage and every moment of this wonderful trip wouldn't have to end anytime soon.

If not ever.

*

They stayed for the full three hours of knitting night, and when they finally left, Ron insisted that they return again the following week. "I'd like that," Kelly said, realizing that even if it hadn't been an activity on her original list, it was one that had surprised her.

"And next time we'll get you to do more than just cast on and off," Ron said, sparking a grin from Evie.

"I'm more of a reader than a knitter when it comes to my escapism. But I'm happy to come for the company."

"Good." Ron grinned and disappeared down the sidewalk, seeming happier than he had when Kelly had first walked into the shop.

"He's a nice guy," Kelly observed.

"My sister—I mean, Hannah—doesn't have much patience for him," Evie said, and Kelly forced away the slight until Evie smiled warmly and said, "But you connected with him right away. That tells me we're kindred spirits."

Kelly liked the sound of it. And she didn't want the evening to end, either. Now that Ron was gone, technically she should be feeling those nervous flutters of being alone with Evie, but they hadn't surfaced yet. "Want to get a coffee or something?"

"Angie's is just across the street," Evie said, and they hurried to the nearest crosswalk, heads bent against the wind. "I love the hot chocolate here, but don't tell my cousin Abby. She's had a competition going with this place ever since she had to convince Bridget to stop serving their pastries and let her take over the breakfasts at the inn."

Kelly laughed. "I like Bridget. And Abby. You're really lucky to have the family you do."

Evie pushed through the door and joined the small line that had formed near the display case. "I am. I never lost sight of that."

"But you thought Hannah did?"

Evie sighed as she studied the remains of the day: a few scones, a lone chocolate chip muffin, and a few cookies that made Kelly think about what she'd learned at the post office.

"I thought Hannah didn't think we were enough. But now I understand that there's always room for more people in our lives."

"Good," Kelly said, grinning, but her smile slipped when her phone started to ring in her pocket.

Lindsay would know better than to call her while she was away on vacation, and none of the places she sent her resume to would be following up in the evening, and probably not this close to Christmas. Unless...her heart sped up when she considered it could be Brian, regretting his decision to dump her for Shannon, once he came to his senses and realized that Shannon was actually no friend at all, devoid of loyalty, and well, basically his moral equal.

No. it wouldn't be Brian. And she should be happy it wasn't.

Except that only left one person. Her father never called her. He was passive that way. Happy to hear from her but never one to reach out.

Meaning it had to be her mother.

Loraine. It was clear as day, on her screen.

"Go on and take it if you need to," Evie said casually as she ordered them two hot chocolates, but Kelly felt her cheeks burn all the same. The woman who had walked out on the sister standing beside her when she was only a baby and had stopped sending birthday cards or Christmas gifts just a few years later was calling her. Had she ever called Evie? Ever reached out? According to Hannah there were sporadic gifts for a while, usually age-inappropriate or not to their tastes, a reminder that she didn't know her first two children at all. And then, eventually, the gifts stopped. And so did all communication.

"It's okay," Kelly said, jamming the device into her bag.

"Oh." Evie's cheeks flushed pink, too, and she didn't need to say any more to show that she understood.

The ringing seemed like it would never stop, dragging out the awkward moment as they collected their mugs and found a seat near the window, and Kelly was afraid to silence the ringer for fear she would accidentally press the wrong button in her state and then connect the call instead.

Finally, after what felt like an eternity, the ringing stopped. Kelly shrugged out of her coat and said, "I'm sorry."

"I'm not mad at you for having a relationship with your mother," Evie said. She hesitated. "*Our* mother." Glancing up at Kelly across the table, she said, "It still feels unnatural to say that."

"I know you weren't happy when Hannah came out to California," Kelly started, relieved that they were finally discussing the topic directly. The only time Loraine had been mentioned was back when Kelly had written to her Ask Evie column about her discovery of Loraine's affair with Chaz. Even then, Evie's view of her mother shone through, when she had no idea she was actually discussing the very woman.

Now Evie sighed. "Loraine made her choices. Hannah

did too. And in a way, I made my choice. I'm an adult. I've chosen not to seek her out. The way I see it, I lived my entire life without her, and it was a good life. I never felt like anything was missing."

Kelly swallowed hard and stared at her drink, wishing that last comment didn't sting as much as it did.

"Oh, Kelly," Evie started, but Kelly just shook her head.

"I understand. You had Hannah. And Chip sounds wonderful. And your cousins…I loved them. And Mimi." She looked her sister in the eye. "Would it be terrible to say that I was a little jealous?"

Evie broke off a piece of the cookie they were sharing. "You really feel that way?"

Kelly shrugged. "I was sort of a lonely kid. I didn't have any cousins or siblings and neither of my parents were around much. Loraine isn't exactly the maternal type," she added, meeting Evie's knowing look. "Except…"

"Except what?" Evie peered at her, as if she knew that Kelly was holding something back, and why shouldn't she? She was a licensed therapist. She had advanced degrees. She was about to become a nationally syndicated advice columnist.

And Kelly had always been a terrible liar. Wore her heart on her sleeve, as Loraine liked to cluck. Apparently, that wasn't a good thing.

"Loraine and Chaz broke up," Kelly said.

Evie looked interested by this. "Who broke up with who?"

Kelly hadn't thought to ask this. "Judging from her reaction, I'd say he ended it. She's acting, well…She's acting the way she gets when she's feeling restless again. She usually starts a new hobby as a way of immersing herself in something other than her feelings."

"What's the hobby this time?"

Kelly gave her a long look. "Christmas, it would seem. She's suddenly eager to have a homey, family Christmas."

"And you're not interested," Evie commented, rather than questioned.

Kelly plucked the small cookie straw that was tucked into the side of the drink from the whipped cream and took a bite. It was still warm, and it melted in her mouth. "Is it terrible to say that I'm not?"

"Like I can talk," Evie said. "The only difference is, our mother is trying with you."

"Oh, Evie."

But Evie just held up a hand. "She made her choice. I've made mine. And I'm happy, honestly, I am. And I'm happy that you're here."

Kelly grinned. "I am too." Happy to be here, in this café. Happy to be here in this town.

And really, she didn't want to leave. Not today. Not for Christmas. Not ever.

*

Kelly had one more stop to make before she retired to

her cottage. She was already dreaming of her fresh flannel pajamas, thick cardigan, and a holiday movie playing in the background while she finished up the last of her stockings.

The lights were on in the big house, and she took the main drive this time, happy that she'd had the sense to carry a flashlight with her, given how dark it was once you stepped away from the lights on Main Street.

Her heart was thumping when she considered what kind of animals might be in the woods. Wolves. Coyotes? If she screamed would Noah even bother to save her? Would he even hear?

She quickened her pace, and by the time she reached the front door, she was out of breath. She took a moment to compose herself before ringing the bell. Murphy's bark confirmed that at least he was home, and as the sounds of the dog grew louder, she could only assume that Noah wasn't far behind.

The door opened to his scowling face. "Yes?"

My, he was a testy one. "Not the most pleasant greeting, but I'll take it," she said, determined to kill him with kindness if it was the last thing she did. After all, she wasn't exactly going to make him believe in the spirit of Christmas if she stooped to his level, now would she?

"It's been a long day," he said wearily, combing a hand though his hair. He looked at with her overt impatience.

"Do you have something on the stove that's burning?" she inquired sweetly.

He frowned at her, finally giving her his full attention. "No. I don't cook."

"Then I don't see what the hurry is," she said. "And pity you don't cook. I bet this house has an amazing kitchen. Back in San Francisco, my counter space is about one square foot, if you can believe that."

She grinned at him, holding it so long that her cheeks started to hurt, but still he didn't budge. "I have a lot of paperwork to get through tonight."

Behind him she could see an ornate banister, a red carpet runner, wallpaper in a heavy brocade print. Hardly the kind of modern décor one would expect to find in a bachelor pad. But then, this was hardly a bachelor pad. This was more like...

Well, it was his grandmother's house.

"I won't keep you, then. I just stopped by because I come bearing a gift." She held out the paper bakery bag she'd reused to hold Murphy's toy.

He seemed to visibly recoil. "I told you. I don't want gifts."

"You told me you don't want cookies," she corrected him. "You never said anything about gifts."

He stared at her. Clearly, she had succeeded in winning that part of the argument.

"Besides, it's not for you," she said calmly. "It's for Murphy. Consider it an early Christmas gift." She grinned down at the sweet little dog face. If she stayed in Oyster Bay, she could get a dog of her own. There would be land for it to run and play. It wouldn't be fair to get a pet in her cramped shoebox of an apartment back in San Francisco.

"How many times do I have to tell you that I don't like Christmas?" Noah asked.

She sighed as she pulled her eyes back up to him. He really wasn't going to budge, not easily at least. "Until you finally admit that you love it," she said, bending down to set the toy at the dog's feet. He sniffed it a few times and then gingerly picked it up in his teeth. After giving her a long, appraising look, he ran off with his new treasure, tail wagging.

"Looks like that was a success," Kelly said, grinning.

Noah folded his arms across his chest. "Look, I'm not like you. I'm not one of those people who grew up having cozy Christmases with tons of presents and good feelings and singing and all that...crap."

She leveled him, eye to eye. "That makes two of us then."

He frowned. He clearly hadn't seen that coming.

After a moment, he shifted on his feet, his stance softening. "How can I get you to stop bringing me gifts?"

She thought about it. She needed to find some way to get him into the holiday spirit, and if gifts delivered to his door weren't going to cut it, then she'd have to try something bigger.

"I promise never to knock on your door with any gifts, so long as you do one thing."

His eyes hooded. "What's that?"

This was a big one, but she figured she may as well go for it. "Come to the Christmas Bazaar with me. It's this Saturday at the town hall." Before he could protest, she said, "Or I might just show up here caroling later on tonight, and I can promise you, I have a voice that will make Murphy howl."

Was that a little bit of a smile she saw tugging at his mouth? After a moment he said, "How long do I have to stay?"

She tried not to register any delight in her expression. Really, she had assumed he'd turn her down point-blank. "An hour," she said, throwing something out there. Surely she could work some magic in an hour, especially if he would be surrounded by Christmas and all its cheer.

He looked down at Murphy, who had returned and set the toy down at Noah's feet, no doubt hoping for a game of fetch. "Fine," he said, starting to close the door.

"Fine?" She could barely believe it. Surely, she hadn't heard correctly.

"One hour," he said. "And no more gifts!"

The door closed before her and Kelly couldn't help it, she dropped into the snow and made a snow angel, right then and there. Let that be another little surprise he found the next morning, she thought with a grin.

Chapter Seven

The town square had been set up as a tree lot for the season, complete with hot chocolate and cider stands, and carolers dressed in vintage clothing. The crowd was thick; everyone was excited for the Bazaar tonight, and tourists had flocked to town for the weekend, making the lines for the cider a little longer than Kelly was willing to stand around for.

Besides, she was on a mission. Christmas was a week away now, and she wasn't going to delay the purchase of a tree any longer.

Her sisters had gotten to the square a bit earlier than her, thanks to some last-minute work on a particularly tricky fair isle stocking that had delayed getting out the door on time. Hannah handed her a steaming paper cup, and the smell of chocolate wafting through the air told her what was inside before her first sip.

"These guys deliver, right?" She hadn't exactly considered how she would get the tree back to the cottage, much less stand it up straight.

"Of course," Hannah said. "For a charge."

Kelly tried not to let herself worry about money right now. It was Christmas, after all, and a special one at that. And tonight she had a gig, a paying gig. If anyone actually bought her stockings, that was.

She pushed aside the doubt that crept in every time she thought about the Bazaar. Last night, she'd had a nightmare that all her stockings had unraveled when people hung them up, and the phone was ringing with people demanding a refund. She'd woken to her phone ringing, only the caller display showed her mother's name instead.

She'd have to take her calls. And she would. But not today. Today she was buying a Christmas tree.

Kelly quickly forgot about the two trees she'd already eyed as she walked through the makeshift forest, surrounded by firs, pines, and spruces. "I can't believe I am going to finally have a real tree."

"You never had one growing up?" Evie asked, and Hannah and Kelly exchanged a knowing look.

"Loraine prefers artificial," Kelly said. White artificial, technically speaking, because it matched the white furniture, white walls, white pillows, and bleached hardwood floors that Loraine felt helped her mind feel free of clutter. That was a trend she had started when she first moved to California, apparently, and as Kelly grew older, it always made her feel shifty. Had Kelly and Hannah and their homey house in Oyster Bay been the clutter she so desperately needed to be free of?

"I never even knew people really bought plastic trees until I spent my first Christmas in California," Hannah remarked.

Kelly felt uncomfortable at the memory. Hannah was in college then, living in the dorm, but for break she was going to stay with them, in Kelly's room. Kelly had asked Loraine if she would make a special dinner, seeing as Hannah was with them, and usually it was just the three of them, since both her parents were only children and there were no cousins. Maybe, she thought, Loraine would make a turkey, or a pie. Maybe they would all watch *It's a Wonderful Life* together, with bowls of popcorn. But Loraine had ordered Chinese that year, and when the movie came on, as it did every year, she claimed she was too tired from the day to watch, and disappeared to her bedroom, leaving the girls alone to watch the movie, which suited Kelly just fine. Every other Christmas, she had watched the movie alone.

She remembered the strange frown that had knit Hannah's brow all day, the desire Kelly had to apologize, to explain, to keep Hannah with her forever, or to go with her, if she ever had to leave. Her biggest fear had been that Hannah would leave and never return. And when Hannah described her wonderful Christmases back in Oyster Bay, complete with sledding and cookie baking and caroling, that fear grew stronger with each story.

And eventually, she had left. Left to never return. Just as Kelly knew she would.

"I asked her once why we couldn't have a real tree." Kelly checked the tag on a fat little spruce, nearly gasping at the price. Maybe this was why they'd had a fake tree, she considered. She moved on, looking for something a little smaller.

"What did she say? Allergies?" Hannah asked.

Kelly wondered if she could even bring herself to say it. "She said she didn't believe in murdering trees for commercial consumption."

Hannah barked out a laugh, but Evie frowned, deeply. "So she cares about some causes then. Just not motherhood. At least, not with all of us."

It was so surprising for Evie to show any vulnerability when it came to Loraine that Kelly didn't quite know how to respond. She looked at Hannah, who just sighed and said, "Loraine cares about everything. Deeply. For a little while. Some things just stick longer."

They moved on to the next row, where trees of more modest sizes were set beside a large stand selling wreaths of all styles, some decorated with dried berries and pinecones, some with just ribbons. Evie and Hannah had explained that they'd already purchased their trees, right after Thanksgiving. Chip took the girls every year, of course, and this year Liam, Dan, and Lucy had joined in for the tradition.

The tradition. Kelly longed for a tradition of her own.

Maybe, she thought, with a surge of hope, this would be it. Christmas in Oyster Bay. Christmas at the cottage. Not just this year, but every year.

"Evie?"

Kelly turned to see Ron staring at Evie, his cheeks a little red and his eyes a little wide, and in his hands, the unmistakable ball of mistletoe.

Evie homed in on it right away. Very little went unnoticed with her middle sister, Kelly realized.

"Hi, Ron," she said pleasantly. "Did you find some mistletoe?"

"Mistletoe?" Oh, Ron was indeed a poor liar. Now his ears looked like they were positively burning. "This isn't…a wreath?"

Kelly felt a laugh sputter on, and Hannah just closed her eyes and stepped to a table of wreaths, leaving Evie to tilt her head and gave Ron a withering look. "It's a ball, Ron. Of mistletoe. Please tell me it isn't what I think it is."

"It's just a gift," Ron said, jutting his chin.

"For Jill?" Evie's voice was kind and patient, but Ron squirmed under the heat of her gaze.

"For…for…Fine. For Jill." He blinked down at the greenery in his hands, and for a moment, Kelly feared he might cry.

Evie's mouth was pinched in disappointment. "Ron—"

"It's not from me!" he blurted, his expression desperate. "I'm going to say it's from...her Secret Santa."

Kelly saw Hannah glance over her shoulder and give her a wide-eyed stare. Kelly bit her lip, hard, and turned away. Poor Ron. Seemed that *Don* would be writing another letter to Evie soon.

"The holidays are hard," Ron was saying, behind her.

"The holidays are a very difficult time of the year for most people," Evie said softly. Oh, she was good. And it was true, so true. It brought out the best in people, but in some people, it brought out the worst.

Kelly thought about Noah, the town Scrooge, and his aversion to the holiday. Surely it couldn't be without reason. Surely something would have caused him to turn his back on the holiday. Something that brought out the worst in him.

She walked down the next row of trees, leaving Evie and Ron to have a heart to heart, her mind hard at work, thinking of what Ron had said to Evie....Minutes passed, and an idea took shape.

She glanced over her shoulder, happy to see her sisters now chatting with each other, deep in conversation as they picked up a wreath. Ron's ball of mistletoe sat on a pile of gold ribbon. The impromptu therapy session had been a success. With only the slightest hesitation, she walked over to the counter and said to the man behind it, "If I were to buy someone a tree, could you deliver it to them for me?"

"Sure," the man said distractedly. "We don't have any

open deliveries until tomorrow though."

"That's fine. And could you not reveal who sent it?" Now she had his full attention. "It's sort of a Christmas…surprise."

That was putting it mildly. She could just picture the look on Noah's face when a seven-foot fir tree showed up at his door. There was always the risk he would refuse it, but who could really refuse a Christmas tree?

"I think that could be arranged," the man said, reaching for an order form. "Who should I say sent it?"

Kelly could barely suppress her excitement. "Let's say, his Secret Santa."

The man grinned at her. "Have a Christmas crush, do you, young lady?"

She felt her cheeks flame. It wasn't like that, not at all. But she didn't have time to explain. Her sisters had finished selecting their wreaths, and she could hear their voices approaching.

"And who is the lucky young man?" The man's blue eyes were kind and patient.

"Noah Branson," Kelly said, waiting for the inevitable reaction.

Sure enough, the man let out a low whistle, but wrote the name down all the same. "Good luck with that one, young lady, but a word of advice if I may. That man doesn't deserve a pretty girl like you, if you ask me. Save yourself the trouble and look somewhere else. All that boy ever did was break hearts."

Kelly swallowed hard, heeding the advice as much as she wished to ignore it, and smiled brightly as her sisters approached, each with their arms looped through a beautiful Christmas wreath.

"Did you pick out your tree?" Evie asked.

"Yep, my order is all placed," Kelly said quickly, but her cheeks felt warm as she glanced at the man behind the counter, who just shook his head knowingly and reached for the wreaths.

"You really like it at the cottage," Hannah said as she set her purchases on the counter.

Maybe, Kelly thought. Or maybe she just liked what it represented. She liked her life here in Oyster Bay. She liked being with her sisters, being included. She liked being in a town where you bumped into familiar faces, unlike San Francisco, where you never saw the same person twice, unless it was your neighbor, and considering hers was an overweight man who didn't like to wear a shirt, she'd happily take a pass.

"You know that Loraine wasn't one for big holidays," she muttered to Hannah. Until now, she thought, feeling uneasy.

"I know," Hannah said a little sadly as she handed over the money for the wreath and collected the bag. "That's why I'm happy you're here with us this year. It's too bad it's just for Christmas."

Kelly was bursting to tell Hannah about the deal she'd made with Noah, but she wasn't so sure she'd entirely approve, and besides, there was no sense in getting ahead of herself. Yet.

"Maybe tomorrow you guys could come over to the cottage and we could bake some cookies," she offered brightly, but she was met with two horrified-looking sisters.

"That cottage is creepy, Kelly," Hannah said, giving her a wary look.

"It's not creepy," Kelly huffed. "It's cozy. Give it a chance."

Evie and Hannah exchanged uncertain glances and finally shrugged. "Okay," Evie said. "If you say so."

Another item on her list, Evie thought. Maybe by the end of the day tomorrow, they could finally pull out that toboggan.

"Lucy's school chorus is performing at the Christmas Eve tree lighting," Hannah said, gesturing to the oversized and fully decorated tree near the gazebo. "And after, we'll all go to The Lantern for dinner."

"We could stop there for lunch," Evie offered. "I could use a bite to eat."

Kelly hoped the panic didn't show in her face. "I need to finish some stockings before tonight." The Bazaar would start in a matter of hours, now.

"But you still haven't met our dad!" Hannah said, pointing to the sign for The Lantern that was visible at the end of Main Street.

Kelly's heart was pounding so hard that she thought it would come out of her body. "Oh, I'm sure he's busy working." She gave a nervous laugh, but Hannah didn't seem to notice.

"I want you to meet him." Hannah's look was imploring, as if this part of her life were something she was eager to share. But was Chip so willing to share it? After all, even Evie hadn't come around to the idea for well over a decade, and they were blood. "It's too weird that my sister and my father don't know each other. I don't like having separate lives."

Separate lives. But that's exactly what they'd always had. All three of them. And hadn't she been the one to stop that pattern? To bring them all together at Christmas?

"You don't think my presence will bring up bad feelings about…" She waggled her eyebrows.

Hannah almost burst out laughing. "That's ancient history!"

"I know." Kelly shifted on her feet. "But I've always felt bad about it."

"You can't be responsible for someone else's behavior," Evie reminded her, and Hannah gave her a lock of mock annoyance.

"You take that line out of your latest column?"

Evie's cheeks flushed. "Actually, I might have," she admitted, laughing. "But really, Kelly, what our mother did, it has nothing to do with you. And my father knows that. And he's also over her. He's had a good life. He's happy."

"And I can't exactly say the same for Loraine," Kelly

sighed. "Man bun broke up with her," she told Hannah.

"How's she taking it?" Hannah's tone was lacking any amusement as they walked down Main Street, where shoppers were browsing store windows, stopping to comment on the elaborate displays, each unique and clearly designed with care.

Kelly stopped to admire the bookstore window, where all the holiday picture book classics were set out. "Oh…" She stopped herself short. She couldn't say that Loraine wasn't taking it well, could she? That she was having some sort of midlife crisis about it, that she suddenly decided to be a hands-on mother?

Hannah wouldn't buy it. And really, neither should she.

People didn't change, at least not that abruptly. Dr. Chandler had told her this. Her heart had told her this. Evie's column told her this.

And yet…Hope. Was it so wrong to hold out hope, especially at Christmas?

Chapter Eight

The Christmas Bazaar was a much bigger deal than either Evie or Hannah had let on, and Kelly made them aware of this the moment they began setting up the booth that Hannah had reserved for her at the back of the room.

"Right near the hot chocolate stand!" Evie said happily. As if Kelly hadn't had enough of it earlier today at the tree lot.

"Half the town must be here," she whispered, as she set the shopping bags full of stockings on the table.

"More like the whole town," Hannah said, not catching the anxiety in her tone. "Well, aside from a few. I doubt Noah Branson will show up."

Kelly widened her eyes at the pile of stockings, happy that her back was to her sisters so they wouldn't see her expression. My, they were in for a surprise.

If Noah decided to keep up his end of the bargain, that was. If not…Well, she'd just have to think of something else.

"Such a shame that Noah went to the dark side," Evie said as she began expertly sorting the stockings into piles by color. "Remember when we were little, how Mrs. Branson used to give away cookies to everyone as they came through the door of the Bazaar?"

"You never told me that story," Kelly said to Hannah. She was happy to hear it, a new piece of information, something she could add to the collection of Hannah and Evie's memories, only this time, she wouldn't have to feel like she was missing out, at least not completely. Now she was here, at the Bazaar, too.

Only not exactly as one of the guests. She looked down at her pile of stockings, wondering how they would compare to the other homemade gifts being offered. The woman next to her was setting up beautiful glass ornaments, each in the shape of an icicle, but all so different in color that Kelly immediately felt cheerful just staring at them.

Kelly supposed she should be grateful to be on an aisle. More exposure and less comparison. It wasn't until this moment that she realized how badly she wanted to sell her stockings, and all of them. Sure, it had been fun making them. A lot of fun, actually, but the truth was that the thought of selling them for money was appealing, enough to make her dream of other things she could sell, too.

"Lucy's girl scout troop is collecting for the raffle and I volunteered to oversee the kids," Hannah said. "You don't mind if I go help them, do you?"

"Of course not," Kelly said. But Evie must have seen the trepidation in her eyes because she lingered a moment after Hannah had spotted the group of young girls across the room and ran off to meet them.

"It's not easy to go after the things you really want. This is the first step. I'm proud of you."

"It's just stockings," Kelly said, glancing over at the beautiful glass ornaments again.

"To someone else, they might be more. I still have my stocking from when I was little," Evie said, her gaze turning wistful. "Our dad still hangs them every year."

"That's sweet," Kelly said, imagining what it would feel like to have a stocking of her own, that carried with it so many memories. "Loraine didn't do stockings. She was a fan of gift bags, though."

It was the first time she had broached the topic of their mother without being prompted, but Evie didn't flinch. "Maybe it falls under the category of it being the thought that counts?"

Kelly considered this. "More like too much Chardonnay."

Evie laughed, and Kelly did too, but she stiffened when she saw a young couple approach the table. The woman was pretty and had a beautiful engagement ring on her finger that caught the lights from the decorations that were draped all over the town hall.

"This is exactly what I had in mind for our first Christmas," she remarked to the guy next to her, who gave them the once-over and then nodded his approval before checking his watch. Clearly, crafts and cookies weren't exactly his thing.

Evie winked at Kelly and then motioned with her thumb over her shoulder that she was leaving. A few moments later, she saw Liam come up to her near the punch stand, greeting her with a kiss on the cheek.

Kelly sighed. She never would have dragged Brian to a holiday event like this, and that was half the problem, wasn't it? All her life she'd gone with the flow, done what was expected of her, or what she thought she was supposed to. What she could do, to get Loraine's attention, to make her approve of just something, somehow.

Brian had looked so good on paper. Tall, handsome, with a degree from Berkeley and a bright future in the tech industry. He still made time to stay in shape. Hit the gym every day. Physical appearance was high on Loraine's list, as, of course, was money. Something Chip didn't have enough of, it seemed.

But Chip had stockings that he packed up and took out every year. And Chip had a house full of two giggling girls. Chip probably made them lunch, too, unlike Loraine, who stuck her on the meal plan at school even though she knew how much Kelly hated the offerings.

Chip probably even wrote notes that he tucked under their turkey sandwiches. "It's easier this way," Loraine would say airily, when Kelly complained about the dry meat and pasty pizza slices offered in the cafeteria. Just like the gift bags were easier than wrapping presents.

But maybe she was being too harsh. After all, the woman had most likely just been dumped. Sure, it was by her lover, a man she should have absolutely never been involved with, but still, maybe it was about damn time. Maybe this would soften Loraine...maybe it would change her.

She could practically hear Dr. Chandler cluck his tongue and then hood his eyes with overt disapproval.

When would she learn? Really, when?

Thinking that her mother would change was right up there with thinking that Brian would come back to her. That he'd somehow transform from the jerk he now was and leave Shannon and her cutesy date nights and ring her doorbell, preferably with several dozen long-stemmed roses.

But then, even if Brian were to come back to her, what would that mean? More dinners at the restaurants where he wanted to go? More ball games on television and more double sessions at the gym, even when she was really tired and would rather eat a frozen pizza on the couch in her sweats?

She wasn't going to have a warm and fuzzy lifestyle like the one she'd been craving with Brian anymore than she'd had it with Loraine. Oh, sure, Shannon might try, with her scented candles and wine and cheese nights with a chick flick, but that wouldn't last.

And really, it was about time she stopped checking on Brian's Facebook page for the photos that Shannon always posted of the two of them. Recently, she dared to think she saw a death in Brian's eyes, a boredom that hadn't been there at first, when it was probably thrilling to sneak around behind her back with Shannon.

She hoped she was right. And she didn't care if it went against the Christmas spirit to think so.

"I'll take these two," the girl said, and Kelly snapped out of her pity party so quickly, it was as if she'd just been shaken from a dream. Carefully she collected the money. Money! The only income she'd had for months was the unemployment check, and that was more like a horrible reminder, a ticking of the clock, whereas this…this was actual earnings. She had made something. Something someone wanted.

Damn, it felt good.

"I'll wrap them for you," she said, carefully taking the two red cashmere stockings and setting them in the simple brown paper bags that she'd decorated this morning, on a whim. She'd always loved to sketch, and with a black pen, she'd made a simple but sweet design in the shape of a Christmas tree, and then embellished it with a gold metallic marker that she'd had the foresight to bring with her, just in case she'd had the urge to send Christmas cards back home.

Home. Just the thought of it made her stomach clench. She didn't want to go home. Not now. Not tonight. Tonight she wanted to stay right here, in this quaint little town, where people actually wanted to buy something she enjoyed making.

"These are stunning!" Beth came over, exaggerated shock on her face as she approached, and Kelly laughed, feeling immediately at ease with the other woman. She was again wearing something a little unconventional, a long corduroy skirts and a cardigan that must have belonged to her grandmother at some point, and though she wore no makeup, her blue eyes were clear and bright and her cheeks were rosy. She was rather pretty, but something told Kelly she probably didn't see herself that way.

A shame, Kelly thought.

"I figured you knew what you were doing, but these are absolutely stunning!" Beth picked up one and set it back again. "Would you let me sell a few in my shop?"

Kelly could barely contain her surprise. "Sell some in your shop?" Beth said it as if Kelly were used to these requests, when in fact, what Kelly had grown used to these past couple of months was far too much frozen junk food and living in elastic-waist pants.

Her life was already so much better here in Oyster Bay.

"Only if you have enough," Beth continued. "These are going to sell fast."

"I can make more," Kelly said. "I'll drop them off Monday?"

"Perfect," Beth said, grinning.

"You're not selling anything then?" Kelly straightened the piles on her stand, now that two stockings had been removed from the mix.

Beth shook her head. "I run the store and craft on the side. It takes a lot to put yourself out here like this."

It did, Kelly realized, and it wasn't something she would have done without her sisters' encouragement. She was still smiling long after Beth wandered off, thinking that at least if she didn't sell out tonight, she had somewhere to take all her leftovers. But as the minutes ticked by, she realized that probably wasn't going to be an issue at all. Her stockings were selling, and fast. A mother with three young children bought five, enough for the entire family, and Bridget stopped by to get three for herself, Jack, and Emma.

By the time Kelly was down to only one stocking, she hadn't even realized how much time had slipped away, but the grunt of a man as he approached reminded her of something else she'd lost track of in the rush of her excitement.

She looked up at Noah, who stood in a navy blue scarf and charcoal wool coat, his hands thrust into the pockets, his eyes shifty. His mouth was a thin line of displeasure, and for a moment, she felt annoyed. She'd been riding such a high and now Scrooge himself had come to kill her joy.

But then she thought of the deal. And the cottage.

Eye on the prize, she thought.

"You came!" she said, grinning. She slid her last stocking to the side of her booth, where it would be on full display. "I'm almost done here. I've been smelling that hot chocolate behind me all night, and would love a mug of it."

He didn't seem to catch the hint. Instead, he frowned at her. "When you said to meet you at the Bazaar, you didn't say you'd be working here."

"There's a lot about me you don't know," she said, looking over to a woman who was approaching the table with a hungry look in her eyes.

"Please tell me you have more of these," she said, picking up the last stocking.

Kelly shook her head. "I'm afraid that's the last of them." Catching the woman's disappointment, she decided to seize the moment. "But I take orders. How many did you need?"

"Four," the woman said, sighing in relief. "Can you have them before Christmas?"

"Of course!" Kelly turned over one of her brown paper bags and handed the woman a pen. "I can have them done by Monday. If you write down your name and contact information, I can call you to confirm they're ready for pick up. Several will be on sale at Beads and Bobbles, too. You can pick up your order there."

Hopefully Beth wouldn't have a problem with that, but if it drove traffic to her store, Kelly didn't see why it would be an issue.

"Thank you," the woman said, scribbling down her name. "I'll take four just like this one. But can I have them in green?"

Kelly made a note next to the woman's information. "Certainly!"

Noah was watching her as the woman walked away; a look of confusion furrowed his brow. Kelly refused to let the smile slip from her face. Let him think what he wanted. No one was going to ruin this magical holiday experience for her.

"That toy for Murphy," he said suspiciously. "Did you make that?"

She nodded once. "I did."

"Hmph. That was…nice." He said nothing more, and Kelly looked away so he didn't see her smile. She'd take that as the second crack in his armor. Now, to go in for the third.

She reached into her bag and pulled out her wallet. "Mind getting me that hot chocolate?" When he didn't immediately react, she said, "You aren't just going to stand here for an hour to put in your time, are you?"

"May as well make myself useful," he agreed. He waved away her money, as she suspected he would. "The drink is on me. On behalf of Murphy."

She grinned and began closing up as he trudged away toward the concession cart. A full till, an empty stand, and a hot chocolate compliments of Scrooge himself.

She'd call that a success.

*

Noah couldn't believe he had agreed to this, and why had he? Oh, that's right, so little Miss Christmas would stop showing up at his doorstep bearing gifts. Well, he'd kept up his end of the bargain. He could only hope that she would do the same in return.

The line was long, and Noah stood at the back, checking his watch. He'd agreed to come, but he hadn't agreed to stay beyond sixty minutes or to enjoy himself either.

He could feel the eyes on him, just like he did every time he came into town, which was only for Murphy recently. Poor dog was getting up there in years, needed pills for his arthritis, for his liver, too.

Noah swallowed back the swell of dread that always accompanied that thought. It had just been him and Murphy for so long. His faithful companion. He'd do anything for that dog. Which was why he was here, he supposed. Kelly had shown kindness to his dog, and that was more he could say for anyone else other than the town vet.

Finally, when he was just about to give up, the line inched forward, and he placed his order, paid, and collected his two hot chocolates, even grunting out an acceptance of the crushed candy canes they offered as a topping. "Only on one," he added quickly. Last year's seasonal cookie had been peppermint, another cliché, he'd claimed. Another holiday favorite, his cousin had informed him gaily.

More like another big seller.

Kelly was already standing, stretching back, the smile on her face nearly as bright as the one in her eyes, when he approached. "Crushed candy canes! How festive!"

"I had a feeling you would like that," he said. She was predictable, or so he'd thought. Now he went back to her earlier comment. Was she really not used to cozy Christmases either?

He was curious, and it bothered him that he cared. She was his tenant, and in two weeks she'd be gone. And that should really be it.

"Just plain for you," she observed ruefully, motioning to his classic hot chocolate, no whipped cream, no fancy garnish.

He didn't even know why he'd bothered, but it kept his arms busy, and he couldn't help it. It was awkward as hell being here.

Picking up on his lack of amusement, she looped her handbag around her shoulder and said, "I've been working all night. I'd love to see some of the other stands."

He could think of nothing worse than walking around this town hall turned…circus…and greeting the townsfolk while admiring their crafts. Once he had liked this sort of thing. When he was younger, Gran put him in charge of standing at the door and passing out cookies for all the people who came to the event. "Don't worry. I tucked one in my coat pocket, just for you," she always said, sensing his fear that he'd run out before he'd had time to grab one for himself.

Now there was a little girl standing at the door instead, and she wasn't handing out free sugar cookies. She was selling tickets for a raffle.

There was something in her eyes, disappointment, he'd guess, judging from the roll of tickets that remained in her hand, that made him reach in his back pocket for his wallet. "How much are those tickets?"

The child's eyes lit up. "Ten dollars each."

Ten dollars each? He tried to hide his surprise. Clearly he hadn't been to the Bazaar in a long time. "Back when I was a kid, tickets were about fifty cents."

"Please," Kelly said under her breath. "You're not that old."

True. But he'd been forced to grow up all too quickly. When was the last time he did something spontaneous, without an end goal, without a calculated risk?

"I'll take ten," he said, and the little girl's eyes popped.

"Ten?" Her smile was wide, and she had space where her incisors should be.

He nodded. "That's right. Here's a hundred-dollar bill."

The smile that remained on her face as she carefully counted out ten tickets and handed them to him made him struggle not to smile himself. He didn't know who the child was. Probably the daughter of one of his old classmates. It had been a long time since he'd taken a good look around town when he dared to stop in.

"You made Emma's day," Kelly said as they walked away, giving the little girl a wink over her shoulder. "She's Bridget Harper's daughter. Do you know Bridget?"

He did. Of course he did. The Harper family was a big name in town. And the fact that he didn't know that the little girl was her daughter was disturbing, reminded him that they were all a community and that he wasn't a part of it, and hadn't been for some time.

"So, she's your cousin then?"

The light seemed to leave Kelly's eyes as she sipped her hot chocolate. "Oh. No. She's related to my sisters. Chip's sister was Bridget's mother. I'm just...I don't know, actually." She shrugged, giving him a smile that wasn't very convincing.

Noah handed her the tickets, eager to change topics. "Do you know what the prize is?"

She looked at him in surprise and then burst out laughing. "You mean you don't?"

He shook his head.

"Then why'd you buy them?" she asked.

Good question, he thought. Clearly, there was nothing in it for him, after all. But something about the little girl, and the sad look in her eyes, made him want to, well, change that. And he had.

"You know, I have a feeling that I'm going to win this bargain we have," Kelly said with a knowing smile.

All at once, his good mood faded, replaced by a harsh reminder of all the things he'd managed to forget for a few moments. "Don't be so sure about that."

"Why do you hate Christmas?" Kelly asked, and for a moment, Noah was caught off guard.

"Let's just say that Christmas wasn't always a happy time in my family," he said. That was putting it mildly. Christmas usually meant that his mother had one too many eggnogs, said things she shouldn't, and made Gran cry and Gramps lose his temper.

"Fair enough, but you're an adult now. You can start your own traditions."

Before he had a chance to respond, an elderly man wearing a bow tie stumbled toward them. Beside him was a woman who was looking at Kelly as if they shared some sort of secret.

"Mimi Harper!" Kelly leaned forward and kissed the woman on both cheeks, and for a moment, Noah was startled. Mimi Harper, named Margaret, actually, had been one of Gran's best friends. He hadn't seen her in years, and he now realized just how many years.

Time passed, he thought, seeing the lines in her face, and the frail way she held onto the arm of the man in the bow tie, but the fire in her eyes still shone through.

"I was hoping to buy two of your stockings for Earl and me, but someone took a long nap—" She took this moment to give an accusatory stare at the chagrined-looking man. "Now it seems you've already sold out!"

Kelly set a hand on Mrs. Harper's arm. "No worries. I'll make you a pair. My gift to you."

Mrs. Harper beamed. "I'm so happy you've finally

come to Oyster Bay, Kelly." Giving Noah the once-over she said, "And maybe you'll have a reason to stay."

Noah wasn't sure if Mrs. Harper remembered him, so he cleared his throat and stuck out a hand. "It's a pleasure to see you again, Mrs. Harper. I'm Noah. Sandra's grandson."

"I know who you are," she said, her expression firm but not exactly unfriendly. "About time you showed up at the Christmas Bazaar. Your grandmother loved the holidays."

Noah stiffened. He didn't like to talk about Gran. It was a sensitive topic, especially in town, where everyone seemed to hold opinions that weren't theirs to have.

"I was actually just leaving," he said, eager to get away. Surely he'd done his time, although he had to admit that it had passed quickly and, dare he say, almost pleasantly. Now, though, the room felt like it was caving in on him. It was too warm, his coat was too heavy, and there was a sickening smell, like cinnamon and pine and chocolate all mixed together.

"Off to dinner then?" The old woman's eyes were sharp on his.

Noah pushed back a laugh, until he realized that she was dead serious. "Just home, I think. The snow's starting to come down again."

"You've lived in Maine all your life and you're afraid to drive in the snow?" Now it was the man's turn to look him square in the eye. "Earl's the name. I never knew your grandmother, but I know a pretty girl when I see one, and this young lady looks like she would enjoy a good steak!"

Now Kelly really did burst out laughing, and Noah felt his shoulders ease. "It was a pleasure meeting you, Earl, but—"

"A good steak and potatoes with hot butter," Earl continued, and Mrs. Harper swatted his arm.

"That's what *you* want for dinner, Earl. Kids these days don't eat that way." For a moment, Noah thought he finally had an ally in Margaret Harper, but she just gave him a patient smile and said, "That lovely Italian restaurant is all decorated for Christmas. Candle lights and everything."

Right. Noah felt like the smile was frozen on his face, and his jaw was starting to ache.

"Thank you for the suggestion," he said, as he managed to join the crowd. Kelly was still beside him, and her cheeks had turned as pink as the candy cane sprinkled on her hot chocolate.

He opened his mouth to make up some excuse, to joke away the exchange with Mrs. Harper and her new husband, but Kelly just casually shrugged and said, "I wouldn't mind some fettuccine."

Noah grinned. He hadn't eaten at a restaurant in downtown Oyster Bay since he'd taken over Keepsake Cookies, and for good reason. But as Earl had said, he couldn't resist the opportunity to spend time with a pretty girl. Especially one as sweet and accepting as Kelly.

*

Contrary to Mimi's suggestion, Noah took her for pizza. "Trust me, it's better than that stuffy place with the dark lighting and candles."

"And romance?" she added, forcing him to look up from the menu. "Don't worry," she assured him with a laugh. "I'm off the market."

"Boyfriend?" He looked back at the menu, his expression unreadable aside from the slight pinch between his eyebrows.

"Ex," she corrected. She opened her menu and closed it again, knowing her order and preferring instead to look around the small restaurant, which was playing up the red and white theme, from the checkered tablecloths to the boxes of faux presents that were piled up near the Christmas tree in the corner.

Kelly suddenly remembered the Christmas tree she had ordered for Noah and had to lift her menu to hide her smile.

"What's good here?" she asked.

"Everything," he said with a shrug. "It's one of the few restaurants that deliver, so I've pretty much tried everything on the menu."

She frowned as she set the menu back on the table and unfolded the napkin onto her lap. "You really don't get out much, do you?"

"I have what you might call, a reputation."

She was surprised he had admitted it. "So I heard," she said, hoping he would elaborate.

"Then I suppose you've heard about my grandmother, and the cookies, and how I ruined her generosity and the spirit of Christmas by turning her small hobby into a commercial success?" He lifted an eyebrow, and she had to wince.

"Well, yes, something like that."

"Look." He leaned across the table, and when he did, she had the sudden urge to pull back. His eyes were deep, firm in their hold on hers, and not unkind. If anything, she felt a strange connection with him, a sincerity in his gaze as he looked her. "It was never my intention to upset these people. I just did what I had to do at the time. What I thought was…best."

"And they see it differently?"

He barked out a laugh that bore no amusement. "You've been in town for a week and you've heard all about me, and I assume none of it was good."

"Maybe you just need a chance to prove them wrong," she said. "Show them that they're wrong about you. You aren't helping matters by hiding in that big house all the time."

"Do you blame me?"

She gave a small smile. "No."

He waited until they'd placed their orders and her wine and his beer arrived before saying, "I grew up with nothing, is it so wrong to never want to feel that way again?"

She frowned. "But…you're a Branson."

He shook his head. "That was my grandparents' money. And their house," he corrected. "I didn't grow up in that house."

"Oh." She was confused. "I just…"

"Assumed?" he cocked his eyebrow. "It's okay. That's what people do. It's natural. I suppose I could say I'm guilty of it myself."

She recalled his comment the other day, about how she spent her previous holidays, the surprise in his eyes when he learned he may have been wrong about her. But was she wrong about him? She didn't think so. She saw a kind man, a quiet man, but a kind one. At first sight, he'd been gruff, unfriendly, even a little rude. And now…Now she was starting to hope this dinner wouldn't be the only one that they shared.

"I haven't asked about your job," he suddenly said, and even though Kelly knew this was the natural order of conversation, she wished he'd stayed true to the Scrooge people said he was and not asked at all.

She rearranged the order of her silverware, avoiding direct eye contact. The man was the owner of a major company and she had been sacked for showing up late to work one too many times.

"Oh, well, I'm in between jobs at the moment. I didn't really love what I did anyway." She stole a glance up at him, but he just shrugged.

"Which was?"

"I worked in the real estate department for a commercial real estate firm." She wiggled her nose. "Next time around, I'd like to find something more…me. Is that indulgent?"

"No more indulgent than taking a job just for the money," he replied simply, and she supposed he was right about that. And she also wondered where he fit in. He grew his grandmother's cookies from a small-town business to a national brand. Was it really all for the money like people seemed to think?

She sat back in her chair, listening to the carol that was playing over the radio that was piped in through speakers in the corner of the room, confused when Noah groaned as the commercial break started. She frowned, and then realized why he had the reaction. Of course. It was a commercial for Keepsake Cookies.

"I happen to think this song is catchy," she said, straining her ear to hear better over the din of the room.

"It's nice of you to say that, but if I never hear that song again, it's fine by me."

"Don't let the guy who came up with it know that," she joked, but his wasn't smiling.

"No issue there. I wrote it."

"What?" She stared at him, trying to make sense of what he was saying. "You write music?"

"I used to play guitar."

Uh-oh. Brian had played guitar, and played it well. She looked across the table at her dinner companion, wondering if this was a sign. As if all the warnings from everyone else hadn't been enough.

"I don't play anymore. It was just something I did as a kid. Then one year, my mom broke it. We couldn't afford another, and I guess you could say I lost the desire to play. My mom had, uh, problems."

Kelly frowned. "But the jingle?"

His gaze turned a little wistful. "It was the last thing I ever played, actually. Around the holidays, Gran sold her cookies in town, and she thought it would be fun to come up with a jingle. One year, I came up with this song, and she had it recorded. Then, when we took the company over, Allie thought we should keep the song going, as part of the brand, to show that we hadn't changed too much. As you can see, that strategy didn't exactly work."

"Do you mind me asking you something? Why *did* you start the company?" she asked. There. It was out. Let him confirm the rumors. Let her head be set straight once and for all.

Noah took a sip of his beer. "You know, that's the first time anyone ever asked me that. I did it because it seemed like the best way to keep my grandmother alive forever. How's that for irony?" He cocked an eyebrow as he brought the bottle to his mouth again.

"I think that's a very good reason to start a company," she said, almost wishing he'd proven everyone in town right so she could officially stop this fluttery feeling that was growing by the minute, and their food hadn't even come yet. "It's too bad that more people don't know it."

"They don't care to know it," he said. "They'd made their decisions about me, just like…" He stopped himself short, clearly changing his mind about what he'd been about to say.

Kelly didn't push. She was having a nice time and the last thing she wanted to do was rile him up, especially if she intended to get him into the holiday spirit.

"Just so we're clear," Kelly said, after the bread basket had been set before them. "You don't have to worry about what Mimi and Earl said."

He looked amused. "Oh? So your interest in having dinner with me tonight is just part of the deal?"

"Strictly," she said, giving him a small smile, but inside she was starting to wonder if that was exactly true. "Besides, I never mix business with pleasure." It was bad enough that she had lost her favorite gym in the break up with Brian. She wasn't about to lose out on the cottage because she let some chemical reaction cloud her judgment.

Noah might not be a true Ebenezer, but he was definitely not a romantic possibility. He couldn't be.

Chapter Nine

Noah was just sitting down with his first cup of coffee for the day when the pounding started. Technically, it was a knock, he supposed, but between the noise and Murphy's barking, it was enough to ruin the bliss of a snowy, quiet Sunday morning.

Maybe it was for the best, he thought. He'd been thinking way too much about his dinner with Kelly, from the moment he'd dropped her off at the cottage until he'd fallen asleep, in front of the television, with Murphy taking up far too much of the couch. He'd woken with a backache, and he'd woken with something else. Something he hadn't felt in so long he couldn't even pinpoint it at first. Hope, he'd finally realized. But for what?

He stared at the pile of paperwork in front of him. Spreadsheets and notes for his meeting with Dubrow Foods this Friday. He'd planned to get a head start, spend the day putting the finishing touches on the contract that had been drafted up by his attorney. The knocking stopped for a moment and then started again, and Murphy wasn't going to let him ignore it.

And maybe he shouldn't. Maybe it was Kelly. And that wouldn't be so bad, unless she was bringing gifts.

Murphy was whining now, showing no signs of letting up, and Noah heaved a sigh and muttered to himself as he walked to the front door. It had better not be a gift. They had a bargain. Crystal clear. He would show up to the event last night if she would stop showing up with ways to entice him into the Christmas spirit. He ran through a string of comments he planned to make when he opened the door. What would it be this time? A pie? A cake? He had to admit that the toy for Murphy had been, well, sweet.

Problem was that he wasn't used to sweet. Didn't know how to react to it. Didn't know how to react to anything about last night, really. It had been rare and surprisingly natural to talk to someone who didn't judge him, but instead, tried to get to know him. Normally he kept people away, didn't even allow the opportunity for questioning. Last night had been refreshing.

But it had only been one night. In less than two weeks Kelly would be gone. And soon thereafter, so would the cottage.

Murphy was barking at the door now, louder when the bell rang. Noah pulled open the door, nearly sloshing the coffee in the mug he held with his free hand, and stared at the person on the stoop.

It wasn't Kelly at all. It was a kid. A teenage boy he didn't recognize, but who clearly knew all about the recluse up on the hill, given the way his eyes rounded and his face went a little pale.

When he gulped, an Adam's apple rolled in his thin throat. "Delivery for Mr. Branson, sir."

"Delivery?" So that was her loop hole, was it? He shifted his eyes past the freckle-faced kid, down the hill and behind the gates, where he could just make out a hint of the cottage. Smoke billowed from the chimney. So she was lighting fires again. He hoped that meant the heating wasn't acting up. He didn't want to have to go down there again, step inside, feel that queasy sensation in his gut that happened every time he crossed the threshold. So much for being a good caretaker of the place.

"Yes, sir. Delivery from Festive Farms."

Now Noah narrowed his eyes. Festive Farms was a tree lot. He knew it because he passed it every day on his way out of town and in again after a long day at the office. *Don't tell me*, he thought, but it was no use. There it was. A tree. Tied up on the roof of the kid's beat-up navy sedan. He didn't know how he'd missed that.

"Who sent it?" he asked, but he was pretty sure he already knew the answer.

The kid pulled a delivery slip from his pocket. "It says it was purchased by, er, your Secret Santa."

Despite himself, Noah felt his mouth twitch. Yep, she'd found a loophole all right.

He looked the kid up and down. Tall, lanky, timid seeming. Probably didn't have many friends. Clearly, confronting Scrooge himself was taking all the courage the poor boy could muster.

Who was he to make his day worse?

Against his better judgment, Noah stepped back from the door, shaking his head. "May as well bring it in then."

The kid looked so relieved that Noah felt a moment of shame. The tree was on the small side, and he directed the boy to the front living room window, where Gran always used to keep her tree, cut fresh from the property each year, at least twice as large and chosen to fill the space to its maximum potential. Noah could still feel the glow on his face when he lay on the floor beneath it, staring up at the branches and lights and ornaments that seemed to glitter and shine and take him far away to what felt like another world, a better world.

The boy set the tree up quickly, and Noah reached into his pocket for his wallet, peeling off a twenty. "You're going to tell me who sent this?"

"I don't know, sir. I just make the deliveries." The boy's eyes were so wide that Noah could only determine that he was telling the truth.

Fair enough. Noah handed him the tip and walked him to the door, feeling his stress level begin to climb when he edged back into the living room and stopped to study the offensive object that now blocked his view of the front yard and the cottage at the base of the hill.

He supposed it served one purpose. And Gran would be happy to see the tree in that window, he admitted to himself.

So fine. He'd keep the tree. But he would be damned if he'd decorate it.

*

Kelly knew that it was ridiculous to be crying over cookies. But she was. She'd managed to keep her voice from showing any disappointment while Hannah explained over the phone why they couldn't stop by to make cookies this afternoon after all. "Our dad had three people come down with the flu," she explained. "Christmas Bazaar weekend, of all weekends! The place will be packed. I'm covering the dining room while Evie mans the bar. You can stop by and hang out if you want!"

As if. She was sure the last thing Chip wanted was his ex-wife's love child showing up on one of his busiest days of the year.

"No, that's okay. I have a lot of stockings to make if I'm going to drop them off at Beads and Bobbles tomorrow anyway," she managed.

"Good. Dinner later then? How about we go for pizza?"

Kelly resisted the urge to inform Hannah that she had already dined at the pizza place, last night, with Noah, and that both the food and the company were excellent, but it would be immature to punish her sister for having a family responsibility to take care of, even though she had thought that she was family, too.

"Sounds great," she said, hanging up, the heaviness in her heart like a big lead ball when she eyed the ingredients set out on the counter.

Really, this was juvenile. As was the thought of baking cookies with her sisters. This was the second time she'd broached the topic and the second time she'd been turned down. Well, she could take the hint.

She picked up a fresh ball of yarn and her bamboo needles and dropped onto the couch. She had only cast on half the stitches she would need for the pattern when there was a knock on the door.

For a moment, she thought it was one of her sisters with a change of heart, but then she realized not much time had really passed. Suspicious, she crept to the window and slowly craned her neck until she had a view through it.

Noah stood on her front porch, jaw set, hands in his pocket, looking rather handsome, if she did say so. Not that she was interested. After all, hadn't she learned her lesson with Brian? Now was the time to get her life in order, not mess it up by adding a romantic interest.

She set down her yarn and walked out the door. She hadn't even managed to get out a greeting when he said, "Did you gift me a tree?"

Ah. So he had received it. She should have known that this would have sparked some sort of a reaction. Thinking quickly, she shrugged and said, "Someone gifted you a tree?"

He folded his arms across his chest, showing that he was having none of her games. "That's right. A tree. Very much like the tree that I see in your window."

Caught. Still, she licked her bottom lip and opened her eyes a notch wider. "Most people have trees this time of year."

"But most people don't send them to others. Anonymously."

Kelly knew he had her there, but as there was no way he could prove it for certain, she saw no reason to budge.

It turned out, she didn't have to. "Are you...are you okay?" He frowned at her, leaning in a little, and it was then that Kelly remembered that right up until he had shown up, she'd been crying. She brought a hand to her cheek and pulled it back. Delightful. Smudged mascara. Well, there was no talking her way out of that one.

"It's silly," she said, shaking her head. She resisted the urge to lick her fingers and scrub at her cheeks. After all, how many times in a girl's life did a handsome man just appear on her doorstep? "My sisters were supposed to come over and bake cookies and they had to cancel at the last minute. I was…looking forward to it."

He rolled back in his heels, his eyes drifted to the big house, as if he had a sudden urge to spring full speed up the hill, away from this uncomfortable situation he'd interrupted without invitation. Really, she thought, it served him right, showing up here, angry at her for daring to buy him a Christmas tree!

She expected him to make an excuse, hit the road, and figured at least he wouldn't be asking her about the tree anymore, but instead he gave her a small smile and said. "I'd offer to bake the cookies with you, but, believe it or not, I do really hate cookies."

"And here I thought you were saying that just to be mean," she said, but she struggled not to smile.

He looked a little ashamed. "That was rude of me. I'm not used to people showing up at my door unannounced."

She lifted an eyebrow. "Touché."

"Point taken." He tipped his head, giving her a boyish smile. He studied her for a moment. "Were you really crying over cookies?"

She brushed a hand through the air. "Don't worry. It's fine. It's just that I came here thinking I was going to have some magical Christmas and do all the things that my sisters got to do and that I missed out on and—"

And well crap. She was crying again. She sniffed, and the most unattractive snort released from her nose, causing her eyes to spring open in alarm.

Brian would have run for the hills then. Any hill. Not just the snowy one that led to the Branson mansion. He didn't "do" emotion. Just like he didn't really do commitment either. Good luck, Shannon, she thought to herself. Really, she had been spared. But somehow, being dumped never felt that way at the time.

She reached into the pocket of her oversized cardigan that was store-bought and not hand knitted (someday!) and pulled out a soggy tissue. "I told you that it's silly."

She glanced at him through watery eyes, surprised to see the softness in his. "I can't help you make cookies," he said, "but…I can help you decorate the tree? Unless you prefer it just with the lights." He motioned to the strings of lights she had just finished wrapping around the branches when Hannah's call came.

She didn't know that tears could dry so quickly. Her blinked at him. No doubt her jaw was slacked. "I'm sorry, did you just say that you would help me *decorate my tree*?"

He shoved his hands into his pockets, looking shifty. "Only if it will make you stop crying. Not because I believe in all this Christmas stuff."

Stuff. A step up from *crap*, which is what she seemed to recall he'd called it last time.

"Of course," she said. "Wouldn't want anyone to think you actually enjoy any of these traditions."

His smile was rueful as she stepped back to let him pass inside. "There are enough rumors flying around town to stop anyone from thinking that."

She tried to fight the smile that was taking over her face and failed. "You know, you're not the Scrooge that everyone says you are."

"Is that what people call me?" For a moment, she was worried she had hurt his feelings, but he just laughed. "It used to be Boo Radley. I'm not really sure which is worse."

"Scrooge," she said, without having to give it much thought. "After all, most people love Christmas!"

"Including you," he observed.

She shrugged as she motioned toward the kitchen. She did love Christmas. At least the idea of it. "Hot chocolate?" Before he could respond, she walked around the counter that divided the living space from the kitchen and removed a carton of milk from the fridge. She found a pot and set it on the stove.

Noah set his coat on the back of a chair at the small table and looked around the room, his hands thrust in his pockets, his jaw set. He seemed decidedly tense in the small house, but given the amount of decorations she'd put up over the past week, she supposed that was inevitable.

"I have to ask," she said, as she poured the milk into the pot and flicked on the burner. "As owner of a cookie company, how can you not like cookies?"

"I used to like them," he clarified. "Gran would invite me up to her house and we'd bake together. She always let me lick the spoon."

Kelly grinned. "Up to her house?"

He looked startled, as if he'd slipped up on something he hadn't meant to reveal. "Well, the house is on a hill."

"Did you live in town?" As the milk started to simmer, she added the powdered chocolate, slowly stirring until it melted. The room immediately smelled warm and inviting, and all her earlier troubles started to fade away.

Except she wasn't so sure it was the hot chocolate that was making her feel better. It was Noah being here, she realized.

"We lived near town, yeah." Noah opened a cabinet and removed two mugs and handed them to her. She didn't ask how he knew where to find them. He owned the place, after all. Still, there was a familiarity there. An uneasiness too. "My mom didn't make much time for things like baking."

Kelly turned off the burner and glanced at him. "That makes two of us." She filled his mug and handed it to him, meeting his eye when her hand grazed his, pushing back the rush of heat that spread through her at the touch. "This is my first real Christmas tree, believe it or not."

"I wouldn't have believed that," he admitted, walking across the small room to it. Boxes of ornaments she'd brought with her in anticipation of this trip were stacked on the sofa, and he lifted the lid of one. "These still have the price tags on them," he remarked.

"I know," she admitted. "This is sort of my first real Christmas."

He looked at her for a moment and then went back to opening boxes. "And here I thought you were the little Christmas queen."

"It's never too early to start making new traditions," Kelly said. "At least, that's what I thought. My sisters seem to have other ideas. They've already had their Christmas traditions. They're not exactly interested in recreating them for my benefit."

"And what were some of these traditions?" he asked.

Kelly hesitated, almost wishing she hadn't even brought it up. She highly doubted that the man who claimed to hate the holiday would do anything other than laugh when he heard her grand plans.

Not willing to say them out loud, she reached into her pocket and handed him the list.

He scanned it, silently, his face without any expression, and then handed it back. "Can't say I ever did any of that myself," he said. "Except the sledding bit. Sort of an after-school tradition for kids around here."

"You must have a few good Christmas memories, though," she said.

He seemed to think about it for a moment. Finally he shrugged. "Maybe one or two."

"A-ha!" She grinned. "Okay, you share yours if I share mine."

He looked around the side of the tree, catching her eye. "Another deal? Fair enough."

Kelly took her time finding just the right branch for her next ornament, a snowflake shape that caught reflection of the strings of lights. "My favorite Christmas was the year that Hannah came to California. I wasn't very happy about being an only child and my doll phase only lasted so long."

"I can say the same," Noah said. "Minus the doll part."

Kelly laughed. "So it was just you and your parents then?"

"Just me and my mom," he corrected. "I never knew my dad, and my mom passed away right after I graduated high school. Then I got Murphy." He gave a little smile at that, but there was a sadness in his eyes.

"I'm sorry," Kelly said, hoping she hadn't overstepped.

He shrugged. "We weren't close. I tried, but…"

She met his eye, wondering if she should even bring up Loraine. Just thinking about her and the phone calls that she still hadn't replied to made her anxious. "I'm not close to my mother either, not really. I can't complain, though, seeing as she left Hannah and Evie when they were so young."

"They know it's not your fault," Noah said.

Kelly considered this. Did they? She knew Hannah and their mother had never clicked, and Evie, well, Evie was still sore about everything, and why shouldn't she be? She picked up another ornament, this one in the shape of a candy cane, and hung it on a low branch, knowing those were often forgotten. The tree was coming out nicely, so much more welcoming than the ones she'd had back home, and she felt a strange knot form in her stomach when she thought of Loraine's invitation, wondering if her mother really meant it. Would she invest in a real Christmas this year, with cookies and a tree and lights and a turkey? And if she did, and Kelly missed it, would she feel bad?

"Murphy saved me in a way," Noah said. "Maybe that was my best Christmas. The first Christmas with Murphy."

Kelly smiled. "What does Murphy do all day while you're at work?"

Noah stopped hanging ornaments to take a sip of his hot chocolate. "Sleeps, I suppose. But when he was a puppy he would ransack the place. Tear up books, magazines, even an armchair I had. Good thing it was secondhand anyway."

"This was at the house?"

Noah shook his head. "College. Then business school."

"An MBA?" She couldn't deny that she was impressed. "I suppose that's why you've had so much success with the cookie company."

"I suppose," he said. "I can't take all the credit, though. My cousin Allie put in her share of the inheritance, and she's a great business partner. We weren't close growing up, but coming together on this helped us bond."

"So it's not all bad then?" Kelly asked hopefully.

"No," he admitted after a beat, "but by January, it won't be my problem anymore."

She frowned. "What do you mean by that? Is Allie taking over?" When he didn't reply, she tried again, "Are you closing the company?"

"Selling it," he clarified. He didn't look at her as he hung another ornament from a branch near the window. "It's what's best."

"For who?" she asked, trying to wrap her head around this new information. One minute the entire town was hating on him for commercializing a local treasure. What would they say now if he turned his back on it altogether?

"For me," he said, glancing at her. "And my cousin Allie."

She wasn't about to let him off the hook so easily. "But you said you grew the company to keep your grandmother's legacy alive."

"And look what I've done instead." He shook his head, cursing under his breath. "I messed up. It's best to shut it down. Hand it over to someone who isn't connected to the family."

"What about your employees?" she asked, recalling the wrath he faced for laying off local workers when he built the factory out of town.

"I suppose there will be some restructuring," he eventually said. "It's all part of it."

"Meaning people will lose their jobs?" Kelly couldn't believe how casual he was being about this. "Right after Christmas?"

"Or before," he said. "I have a meeting on Friday to go over the last-minute details with the buyer."

"Friday is Christmas Eve," she pointed out.

His mouth cracked into a little smile. "It's still a business day, Kelly."

Kelly was holding two ornaments in her hands, but she had lost the desire to hang them. It was as if the Christmas cheer had been sucked right out of the room, by Scrooge himself. People were right about him, she realized. Anyone who could let people go right before the holidays was, well, a world-class jerk!

"What?" he asked, cracking open a box of more ornaments. They were Kelly's favorite. Metallic red bulbs that she should be pleased hadn't been crushed in transit, but she wasn't happy about anything at the moment.

She stared at him, probably more like glared at him, and he shook his head, leveling her with a firm expression. "This is a business, not a charity."

True, all true, but still heartless. "If you're able to sleep at night," she said, scooting past him to the other side of the tree so she could hang ornaments near the mantle. And away from him.

"It's not personal," he insisted.

"If you say so," she said, sniffing. Rat bastard, she thought. Who went around sacking people the week of Christmas? No doubt half of them were looking forward to their Christmas bonuses, too. Or depending on them.

"Great, so you think I'm some sort of Scrooge too now, I suppose?"

"I didn't say that," she said. *Ebenezer*, she added to herself.

His voice rose in defense. "I'll have you know that I give to charity. I am, actually, a very charitable person."

"What charities?" she asked, dropping her hands at her sides. She blinked up at him, prepared to wait all day if she had to.

He froze. "Excuse me?"

"What charities?"

His shoulders slumped. A sure sign that he hadn't been completely honest. "The company gives to various children's programs," he said.

She kept her expression blank. Run of the mill. Not impressed.

"And I—"

Oh, this would be interesting!

"I give to the rescue shelter where I got Murphy."

She felt the hard block of ice in her chest thaw, a little. The man had a heart. Somewhere deep in there, underneath that cool, rough exterior, the man was capable of love.

"Well," she said, giving him a side glance. "I suppose that is a nice thing to do."

"Doesn't begin to pay back my end of the deal," he said, the defense seeping out of his tone. "Murphy's the best thing that ever happened to me."

Aw, damn it. When he said things like that, how could he expect her to stay mad at him, even if he was, unfortunately, turning out to seem like the Scrooge people thought him to be. "I don't mind walking Murphy for you, while I'm in town."

He frowned at her, but she could tell he wasn't going to protest too much. "No. I couldn't impose."

"It's not an imposition. I love dogs and I have the time."

"Murphy would probably like that," he said. "He, uh, has arthritis. The medication helps and in the snow he runs like a puppy. But I don't want him to overdo it."

She saw the concern in his eyes and gave him a reassuring smile. "Not a problem. I'll keep things slow and short. Maybe a little game of tug with the rope toy."

"You're being very nice to me," Noah said, looking at her suspiciously. "Why?"

She opened her mouth to say exactly why, because it was Christmas and at Christmas, that's what you did, because she saw someone who was hurting, and maybe misguided, and she wanted to help. Because for reasons she couldn't explain, and which would probably not be understood by anyone in this town, her sisters included, she liked him. A lot. Too much, in fact.

But instead she just said, "It's part of our deal."

"No it isn't," he shot back.

She frowned. "What? Yes it is." The deal. That's all it was. All it could be.

"Being nice isn't part of the deal. The deal was that you will get me to find my Christmas spirit by the day." He frowned at her, but all she could was burst out laughing.

"Oh, Noah. I have a lot more work to do with you than I thought."

But she had time. Not much time, but still, enough. Hopefully.

Chapter Ten

Six inches of fresh powder fell over the night—great conditions for skiers, and bad for drivers. Noah checked the clock on the dashboard of his truck as he swerved into the spot reserved for him, right near the front door of Keepsake Cookies.

Damn. Half past eight, meaning most people would just be settling into their desks, making the long walk to his office that much slower. People tended to look up when he walked past, or look away. Sometimes he didn't know what was worse.

Heaving a sigh, he climbed out of the truck and walked the ten feet on the salted sidewalk to the revolving doors of the office building whose lease ended at the beginning of March. He'd been dodging calls from the building management for going on four months now, stalling when they sweetened an already good deal on the renewal. He was up to six months of rent abatement on a five-year lease extension, but he wasn't in a position to sign anything right now. It would be up to Jerry Dubrow to decide if they continued to use this space, or move the staff over to their headquarters in upstate New York. Or...

He didn't like to think of that scenario. He hadn't thought of it at all, truth be told, until Kelly had to go and guilt trip him last night. Now, as he walked to the elevator bank, he felt dodgy and untruthful, when all that he was doing was running a business, right?

Wrong. At least, that had been what the locals said when he closed the small operation in Oyster Bay and hired more experienced staff in their place. A business couldn't run on housewives mixing dough out of Gran's house. A business needed marketing, and product development, and a budget if it was ever going to grow.

A middle-aged woman he recognized from the product development department called out just as the elevator doors were starting to close. She waved her arms, her smile hopeful, and oh, it was hard to resist the urge to press the button to close the doors once and for all.

Instead he pressed the opposite button, the one that would open the doors, and she jogged in, boots over her suit pants, dress shoes in hand, panting happily. "Meeting started two minutes ago."

"The roads are bad this morning," he agreed. He tried

to summon her name. Linda. Melinda. Mandy. Mindy.

"I'm Cindy," she said, holding out a hand.

Cindy! "Product development," he said, giving a firm shake.

She seemed pleased by his comment. "We have a meeting scheduled with you for the first week of January for some of our Valentine's ideas!"

Ah, yes, Valentine's Day. Another holiday he could neither relate to, nor get excited about, considering his romantic prospects these days were limited to the office and the town he lived in, and neither were options. And Kelly, he reminded himself firmly, was not an option either. Still, he'd supported the Valentine effort, seeing as it was a big seller. People loved the cookie bouquets. The margins on those were nearly as strong as the cookie ornaments and limited-edition gingerbread kits that they had already sold out of for this season.

"I look forward to hearing your ideas," he said, thinking that he wouldn't be here long to hear anything. Would the ideas be pitched to the new owner of the company? Would there never be a meeting at all? Would Cindy have to worry about traffic and road conditions on her way into the office, or would she be at home in two weeks, watching daytime television with a third cup of coffee in her hands?

"Any special plans for Christmas?" Cindy asked.

Noah lifted his eyes to the numbers above the elevator doors. They were only on the third floor. Why had he chosen an office on the seventh? Product development shared the floor.

"Nothing special, no," he said tightly. Not wanting to feed into the concerned look that seemed to crease the corners of her eyes, he said, "How about you? Anything special in your household?"

"Oh, no," she shook her head, blowing out a sigh. "My husband's been out of work since his stroke in October. Thank you for the card, by the way," she glanced at him, fighting for a smile, and Noah blinked in surprise.

A card? He didn't even know Cindy's last name, much less that she had a husband who had recently suffered a stroke. His assistant was constantly bringing him things to sign, and he signed them, quickly, never really giving much thought unless it was a contract or a bill.

He swallowed hard, muttering something under this breath.

"So, it will be quiet for us. Just the two of us. Our daughter's in college in Maryland. We'd hoped to fly her home for the holiday, but fares are so expensive this time of year, and with tuition bills piling up, well…" Another brave smile.

Noah was starting to sweat. He unraveled the scarf at his neck, just as the elevator doors finally slid open and deposited him and Cindy onto the top floor of Keepsake Cookies.

Cindy was already half jogging down the hall to the meeting, and Noah walked a little slower to his office, taking in the sounds of the office, the ringing of phones, the low-voiced conversations, the typing at keyboards.

"There you are!" his assistant said as he passed her desk. "I was worried about you when you weren't here this morning!"

"Worried about me?"

"The roads are icy," Meryl explained, giving him a kind smile.

His stomach was starting to hurt. Meryl had been his assistant from the very first day they'd moved into this building. She was one of the first people he'd hired, and he had the sinking knowledge that she would be one of the first to be let go. What would her role be without him to assist, after all?

He glanced down at her Christmas tree, noticing that one of the ornaments had broken in the near fall last week. "Meryl, I accidentally knocked into your tree and broke an ornament. I'll replace it."

She brushed a hand through the air. "This old thing? It's not expensive. It's just something to cheer things up around here. Bring a little Christmas spirit to the work day."

His smile felt thin. His office door was half ajar. Escape was within reach.

"I hope the roads clear up by tonight. A few of us are planning on going to dinner tonight. Sort of a little Christmas party," she said, glancing out the window. Her eyes were large when they slowly slid back to him. "You're welcome to join us…"

He saw the relief in her eyes when he shook his head. "It's a busy week. I'll probably be putting in extra hours tonight."

"Of course. If you need me to stay late…" She seemed to stiffen in anticipation of his reaction, and started straightening piles of paperwork on her desk nervously.

He held up a hand. "Go. Have fun." After all, it wasn't like he had ever hosted an office Christmas party. Parties cost money, and they also cost time. People drank too much and showed up hung-over, if they showed up at all. He'd learned that right out of business school, when he'd been a low-level manager at a major retail brand in Manhattan, and he knew then and there that if he ever had a business, he wouldn't tolerate it. Offices were for working and parties were…personal.

And there was nothing personal about Keepsake Cookies, he thought, even as his eye caught a picture of Meryl with a young girl.

"I never knew you had a daughter," he remarked. He always thought she had a son.

Meryl stifled a laugh of surprise and blinked up at him quizzically. "Mr. Branson, we've worked together for over five years!"

"I know," he said stiffly. And he did know. Six years ago had been the worst Christmas of his life, even worse than all the Christmases from his childhood, with the arguments and tension, because six years ago was when he'd gotten the phone call that Gran was gone. Gramps had passed the year before, and Gran had insisted that she was fine, she had her community, her cookies, that he should stay in New York. Make something of himself.

A few months after her death, he'd tried to do just that.

He swallowed the bitter taste in his mouth, pushing away the memory of coming home to that big, empty house, with the Christmas tree in the window, all decorated and ready for a holiday that would never happen. Allie and her parents had driven in for the funeral. And then…then everything changed. And all his time, energy, and heartache was poured into Keepsake Cookies.

He sometimes wondered how much different things would have been if he'd just gone back to New York instead.

"Danny made me this picture frame and I promised to keep it on my desk and show off her hard work. One of the homemade holiday gifts they make for parents and present at the class party," Meryl was saying. She smiled at the picture of the little girl, who was dressed up for a dance recital in a pink tutu and tights.

"That must have been fun," he said tightly. Danny. Of course. He'd assumed it was a boy, but now he realized it was short for Danielle. He had been listening, but not close enough.

"Oh, I wasn't able to attend. That was the day we had a meeting with Dubrow," she said.

He stared at her. She hadn't mentioned her daughter's

party. Hadn't asked for the time off. Or had she? Now he vaguely remembered her coming into his office a few weeks ago, asking about a Friday afternoon and leaving early, and before she could get any further, he had launched into questions about the lunch that needed to be catered for the meeting.

People were right. He really was a Scrooge.

"Hold all my calls today, Meryl," he said as he walked into his office. It was reckless, perhaps, even unprofessional, and Jerry Dubrow could call, so might Allie, or one of the attorneys involved in the deal. "I have a lot to catch up on today before the…" He almost slipped and said buy out. Instead he said, "holiday."

"Yes, sir," Meryl said, turning back to her computer screen.

Noah closed the door behind him with a pounding heart. He hung his coat on the hook and sat down at his desk. Outside the window, the snow continued to fall, flakes swirling in the air, covering the hoods of cars in the parking lot below.

It wasn't personal, he told himself. But it was. It always had been. This was Keepsake Cookies. And somehow, it had all gone terribly wrong.

*

Beth was helping a customer select stationary when Kelly pushed through the door, holding two bags of stockings, plus the four she'd promised to the woman at the Bazaar.

"I'll let you consider these all for a moment," Beth said, leaving the customer with a stack of cardstock in a variety of pastel colors. She eagerly reached for the bags Kelly carried and peeked inside. "I'm going to put six of these in the window display," she told. "I already made room for them."

Kelly could hardly believe it. Her stockings, in the window on Main Street, for everyone to see? She set the bags on the counter and watched as Beth pulled each one out, finally selecting her favorites: two ivory snowflake patterns, two red and white fair isle, and the winter green tree stockings that Kelly had just finished this morning.

She followed Beth to the window display, which was set up with balls of yarn and yarn-wrapped gift boxes, and small rag dolls and stuffed animals in knitted sweaters. In the window, she'd hung a new sign, saying "Have yourself a cozy little Christmas." Kelly smiled. That was exactly what she'd planned on doing, wasn't it?

"Everything okay?" Beth asked, glancing at her as she climbed onto her step ladder. She handed Kelly five of the stockings as she began hanging the first.

"Oh, of course. Fine. Never better!" The truth that Christmas was now only five days away, and she still hadn't called her mother back. She knew she shouldn't feel guilty, after all, they had no plans when Kelly had made hers, and she was a grown adult, well within her rights to have her own holiday.

So why did it feel like she was sneaking around behind

her mother's back?

Kelly handed Beth another stocking, forcing her back to the present, to the wonderful fact that her troubles were thousands of miles away, and that she was here, in this snow-covered town, in a shop that was selling her knitted stockings.

"Looks good?" Beth stepped off her ladder to admire her handiwork once all the stockings were hung.

"What about the things you make?" Kelly asked. "Don't you want to feature them too?"

"Oh, not for Christmas." Beth shook her head and folded her ladder. She carried it back to the counter and propped it against a wall, darting her eye to the woman who was still considering the stationary options, before motioning Kelly over to her. Without a word, she opened a drawer, revealing three beautiful tiaras and some matching necklaces.

"You made these?" Kelly hadn't been into princesses since Loraine nixed that phase at the age of four with a lecture about the difference between fantasy and reality that Kelly didn't realize for a long time was a reflection of her mother's own unhappiness. She almost didn't dare to touch the sparkling creations, but she had a sudden desire to try each item on and twirl in front of a mirror.

"It's just a hobby," Beth said, starting to close the drawer.

"They're not for sale?" Kelly reached down to pick up a necklace before Beth could stop her. It was made of crystals that seemed to catch the lights at every angle, some small, some large, some of different shapes. Her use of color was excellent, with a fine balance between the clear and colored gemstones, and Kelly could only imagine the time and skill that went into creating each pattern.

"Oh." Beth looked flushed and pulled at the long braid that dropped over her right shoulder. "I don't think anyone would want to buy this sort of thing. It's just costume jewelry."

"My sister would," Kelly said. "Lucy wants a tiara for Christmas and these are nicer than the ones they sell at Bayside Brides. I'll tell her about these. In fact, you should see if you can sell these at their shop."

"They order that stuff on wholesale," Beth explained in a rush.

Not a good enough excuse in Kelly's mind. "I bet that's only because they have to. Your jewelry would be perfect in their shop. And wouldn't a bride prefer a custom necklace for their special day?"

"Well, when you put it like that…" Beth chewed her lip and stared down at the glittering drawer and then looked at Kelly firmly. "I'll think about," she promised, and from the light in her eyes, Kelly knew with certainty that she would not only think about it, but that she would dream about it. Just like Kelly was still dreaming about the stockings she would knit, and what might come after that: baby blankets and toy sets, scarf and mitten sets, sweaters and cowls.

But none of that was possible if she went back to California. Back there she had an empty apartment she would soon no longer be able to afford, and only the hope of finding another soulless office job to pay the rent. She could make a choice, she realized, not just about how she was going to spend Christmas, but how she was going to spend her life.

With a lightness in her step, she left Beth to help the customers who were now gathering in the shop, some commenting on the beautiful window display, and a couple even asking about her stockings. It was almost time to give Murphy his first walk of the day, and she hurried up the drive to the big house, which looked considerably less foreboding in the clear light of day, but still sterile and unwelcoming.

The Christmas tree was in the window, a dark shadow where something bright and festive should stand. The front door was without a wreath, and the house felt cold and lonely. Murphy was waiting for her, sniffing at the back door as she retrieved a key from under the mat and turned the lock. He let out a bark of excitement when she secured his leash to his collar, and happily followed her outside.

It was a sunny day, making it feel warmer than it was, though Murphy didn't seem to mind the cold. She wrapped the leash around her wrist and thrust her hands into her pockets, letting the dog explore at a contained distance while she took in the view.

There was the cottage, at the far end of the property, and there was her tree, shining in the window. She turned back to the big house, wondering if she dared to push her luck, and decided that with less than a week to go, she would just have to take the risk.

"Come on, Murphy," she said, leading the dog back toward the rear door. "We have some work to do."

And something told her that somewhere in this old house, the spirit of Christmas was long buried, waiting to be rediscovered.

*

Noah could see the house from the road, and that was saying something, considering that the thick pines were even more dense than usual, thanks to the heavy snow weighing down their branches. At first he thought he was seeing things, that he'd fallen asleep at the wheel and was dreaming, of a time and a place that he'd managed to forget, somehow.

But no, it was real. All of it. The strings of lights were wrapped around the front boxwoods, and the gilded wreath that Gran had carefully packed away every January was hung from the front door.

Lights shaped like candles were centered on every windowsill, and through the window he could see that the banister was wrapped in the velvet ribbon that he had assumed had been thrown away years ago. And there, in the big front window, lighting up the night sky, was the tree. Flickering and sparkling as bright as any star, just like it had been all those years ago, when he'd look out the cottage window and up the hill and see that tree shining in the distance, calling to him, inviting him in.

He didn't want to be that boy anymore. Didn't want to feel those thoughts, recall those memories. Didn't want to go back to that dark place when something as simple as a tree with lights could feel like an answer, or a beacon of hope.

He didn't even realize that his teeth were clenched until his jaw started to ache and he pulled his truck to a quick stop, slamming the door behind him as he jogged to the back door. Murphy was in the kitchen, where he liked to spend most of the day, on his bed near the radiator, curled up with his favorite squeaky toy shaped like a monkey.

On the island counter was a plate of biscuits shaped like dog bones, and a note mentioning soup on the stovetop.

Noah walked to the range, where sure enough a large pot was sitting on the back burner, a lid covering the pot, barely masking the smell of rosemary and chicken. It was still warm to the touch, meaning Kelly must not have left long ago. He couldn't help but smile. It had been a long time since this house smelled like anything other than frozen pizzas and take-out. Too long.

Murphy craned his neck and sniffed the air, and Noah gave him a good firm pat behind the ears.

"She's pushy," he said. But damn it if he hadn't come

to sort of like it.

He should be angry. Really angry. He should march down to that cottage right now and tell her the entire deal was off. The cottage. The checking on Murphy. The little Christmas gestures that he hadn't asked for, or invited into his life.

Instead he walked down the hall, Murphy one step ahead, as if eager to show off the shiny new addition to the house, his tail wagging along with his tongue, happily panting as he led the way into the living room, where the tree stood grand and tall, lit up by a thousand lights, the very ones that he used to stare at as a boy, from the bottom up.

The ornaments were hung, the boxes packed away, as if some magical elf had popped in and out, without leaving a trace.

And maybe that's what she was, he thought, thinking of Kelly.

Someone who popped into his life. And someone who would be leaving again.

Just like they all did.

Chapter Eleven

There were two texts and one missed call from Loraine when Kelly reached for her bag the next day. She'd been glued to the window all morning and most of last evening, too, waiting to see if the lights on the tree in the big house would go out, if the headlights of Noah's truck would fill her small living room. But the lights stayed on, and Noah never came down the hill to complain about the beautiful decorations she'd found in the attic and set up throughout the rooms—decorations that had lit the house and brought it back to life, right up until the moment he promptly turned everything off again, at six thirty sharp, an estimated two minutes after she watched his car pull to a stop.

She set down her knitting and stretched her fingers, then her back. Beth had called first thing this morning to ask for another order of stockings by tomorrow, saying that now people wanted to stockpile for next year, or give them out as gifts. Kelly could only assume that if she stayed much longer, she might actually be able to make a thriving business from her hobby, something that felt almost so surreal, she had to wonder if she was overestimating the possibility. But with Beth on her side and the sales steady, it felt like more than a dream. It felt like a reality.

A knock at the door pulled her from her daydreaming. She opened the door, bracing herself for the sight of Noah coming to reprimand her, but she was happy instead to see Hannah.

"I got the weirdest text this morning," she blurted out.

Kelly quickly let her in from the cold and closed the door against the howling wind. She moved the balls of crimson cashmere blend yarn off the seat cushion of the armchair as her sister shrugged out of her coat.

"Aren't you supposed to be at work?" She didn't wear a watch, but when she'd checked her phone a few minutes ago, it had been after eight.

"I'm on assignment this morning," Hannah said, dismissing her concerns with a brush of her hand. She dropped onto the chair. "Please tell me you have coffee. I'd ask for something stronger, but I have to drive out to the lighthouse to get a wide shot of downtown. I swear, the Main Street renovation is the only thing that makes news some days."

Kelly walked to the kitchen and checked the tea pot.

Still warm. "I only have instant," she said.

"That's fine," Hannah said distractedly. She stood up and began wandering around the living space, stopping to admire the tree and then the mantle, where Kelly had yet to hang the three stockings for each of them. "You know, this place is actually sort of cute."

"Don't sound so surprised," Kelly said, pulling two mugs from the cabinet. "I wouldn't have stayed put otherwise."

"I shouldn't have questioned your judgment," Hannah said. "But when you grow up here, well, let's just say that the Bransons have a reputation."

"Because of the cookie company?" Kelly shook her head. "I'm aware."

"That, yes, but because of Gina Branson. When I thought of you staying here, in this cottage, well, everyone still remembers it how it used to be, I guess."

"Who's Gina Branson?" Kelly asked. She checked the fridge, frustrated to see that she was running low on milk. Maybe she could hitch a ride back into town with Hannah.

"Sandy Branson's youngest child and only daughter. Noah's mother. You didn't know he had grown up here?" Hannah shrugged. "Weird. But then, he was always too quiet, that one. Most people in town pitied him. Until, well. The cookie company."

"Noah grew up here?" She looked around the small space, remembering his comment about going up the hill, about growing up with nothing. About his troubled mother. No father.

"You could hear Gina Branson screaming from the end of this drive. They say she drank too much. Sandy tried to get her help. Tried to take in Noah, too. In the end, she did all she could for him. Put him through school. Left him the house. Gave him more than half of everything, and the rest to her other grandchild."

Allie. Noah had mentioned her. But why hadn't he mentioned that he had grown up here? And why would he want to tear down his childhood home?

"Anyway, it's not nearly as bad I assumed it would be. And you made it so cute and festive. I guess that's why I don't understand…You're going back to California for Christmas?"

Kelly stopped stirring the milk into the mugs of coffee and stared at her sister. "What are you talking about?"

Hannah frowned. "I got a text this morning. From our mother. You can imagine my surprise!"

Kelly could. From what she knew, Loraine and Hannah hadn't really been in contact since Hannah left town to travel South America before returning to Oyster Bay. They'd never gotten close, but then, Loraine struggled to be close to anyone.

"I don't know what you're talking about," she said quietly. She handed a mug to Hannah.

"Loraine texted. She said that she wants to have a big family Christmas this year and that you already knew about it and now she was telling me." Hannah hadn't mentioned Evie, and Kelly could assume this meant that she hadn't been included in the invitation. Growing up, it had been as if Evie and Hannah never existed, or were distant cousins, until Hannah arrived in town.

"I'm not going home for Christmas," Kelly said. "I'm here. In Oyster Bay." But something in her tone must have wavered, the guilt, met with doubt, that she was finally about to have an unfulfilled childhood fantasy brought to life and she was going to miss it.

Hannah studied her for a moment. "If you want to go back, I'll understand. She's your family."

She was both their family, but Kelly didn't want to get into technicalities. "You're my family. This year I wanted to spend the holiday with this side of the family."

"I just don't want to feel like I'm keeping you from anything," Hannah said as she sipped her coffee.

"From plastic trees and store-wrapped gifts and take-out dinners?" Kelly shook her head. "No thanks."

"That's not what Christmas is about," Hannah said, and Kelly shot her with a look that silenced her.

"Easy for you to say, growing up here in this winter wonderland," Kelly remarked. She stared at her coffee mug, wondering why she'd bothered to make it. She usually had one cup a day, two if she really needed it, and she'd only made the extra mug so she could share a coffee with her sister.

"Whoa, where is this coming from?" Hannah frowned, and for a moment Kelly felt bad. Hannah wasn't the real source of her frustration. Loraine was. But Hannah should know that. She was her sister. She should understand. If she didn't, who else would? "I'm just saying that Christmas isn't about the food or decorations. It's about being with family."

Like she was one to talk! "Are *you* planning on going back to California for Christmas then?"

"Of course not!" Hannah looked almost amused.

"And if I were still there, would you have come back?" Now Kelly's heart was beginning to pound, and she could feel the hurt creeping into her voice, and even though Hannah hadn't answered her yet, she already knew. Hannah wouldn't have come back. Because no matter what she said about family, in her mind, her family was here.

"Kelly," Hannah started, but Kelly walked to the sink and dumped the contents of her mug down the drain.

"I don't know what I was thinking," she said. "These are your traditions. Your family traditions. Not mine."

"But you're my family," Hannah said, trying to reach for Kelly's arm as she pushed past her toward the couch. Her knitting was in a pile on the window, a stocking half finished, five more to go by the morning meant she'd have to be quick. Or maybe she'd just use the three she had stowed away, the three that were meant to be for them. The sisters.

"You have an entire life here, Hannah. I don't know what I was thinking, trying to become a part of it." At the end of the day, she'd go back to California, Hannah would stay here. Evie, too, of course.

What had she been thinking trying to strike up a deal with Noah, trying to make something out of nothing, insert herself into a community and a family that was already full?

"I want you here," Hannah said. "Evie wants you here."

"Does she?" She knew that wasn't fair, but she couldn't push aside the hurt she felt that it had taken Evie this long to want to even know her. She shook her head. "We have to face it. You have your family here, and I have my family there. And as nice as it would be to mix things together, it doesn't always work that way. You should know. You never plan to come back to California again."

It was a statement, not a question, and Hannah didn't bother to argue. She cast a sigh into her coffee as she looked down at her mug. "I want you to stay for Christmas," she said.

Kelly swallowed the lump that was forming in her throat. She'd wanted to stay for Christmas, too. Even beyond Christmas.

But maybe she'd wanted too much. Or maybe what she'd always wanted just couldn't be found.

*

Noah had been woken that morning by a call from Allie, something that rarely happened outside the office.

For a moment he was brought back to that last year of Gran's life, when he was in New York, when she was here alone, and he was worried, on edge every time the phone rang.

"Hello?" His heart was pounding as he sat up in bed, and he had to force himself back to the present. There was no more bad news to deliver. Gran was already gone. Soon, the last memories of her would be too.

His stomach had a burning sensation, one that was growing stronger every day leading up to the big meeting with Dubrow Foods.

"Jerry sent over some last-minute changes to the contract last night." Allie's tone was clipped. No doubt she was already at her desk. Perhaps in her pajamas, but still at her desk. Probably on her third cup of coffee too.

"And?" Noah pushed back the covers on his bed. Beside him, Murphy stirred, and Noah transferred the call to speaker so he could toss on a sweater and get the dog outside.

"They're looking to move all operations to their Cleveland facility."

"Cleveland!" Perhaps sensing his alarm, Murphy let out a loud bark. Noah led him down the stairs and attached his collar. When he opened the door, he didn't even care that he was barefoot and that the wind was howling, blowing up the snow in gusts. "Keepsake Cookies isn't from Cleveland."

It was from Oyster Bay. From this house. This kitchen, in fact.

"Those are the new terms. I see no reason not to accept them," Allie said briskly.

Really, there was no good reason not to accept the terms. Consumers didn't care where the cookies were made. They cared about taste, price point, even packaging.

"I think we need to meet before Friday," Noah said. They were far along in the process, there was no reason to back out now, except that's what he suddenly wanted to do. Cleveland! "I'll drive in to Boston today and get a hotel for the night."

"If you think that's necessary." Allie sounded surprised. In the past, she always came to Maine, to the office, not his house. Gran's house.

"I do," Noah said. He needed to clear his head. Needed to talk this through. Needed to be sure he was doing the right thing, long term.

He'd made enough mistakes. He couldn't make anymore.

*

Kelly had just finished taking her frustration out on one stocking and was casting on for the next, when she saw Noah's truck pull up outside the window. Of course. He'd come to complain, to tell her not to bother checking on Murphy, which she'd planned to do in about thirty minutes, to tell her that the deal was off, that there would be no saving the cottage. It was just a matter of time, and she should have known better than to expect anything otherwise.

She set down her knitting and grabbed her borrowed winter coat from the small closet near the door. She was outside on the front porch before Noah was even out of his truck.

From the look on his face, he wasn't happy.

"You decorated my house yesterday," he said. His boots crunched in the snow as he closed the distance between them, but for the first time since she'd met him, Kelly wasn't up for an argument.

"You're right, I did. I shouldn't have done that." Maybe she shouldn't have done any of this. Maybe she shouldn't have even come here at all.

"Kelly—" he started to say, but she just shook her head. Her coat was unzipped and the wind was rushing through the opening. She folded her arms across her chest in an effort to keep warm, but it was no use.

"Forget it, Noah," she said. She didn't need a lecture, and she sure as hell didn't have the energy to try to help him find the spirit of Christmas when she couldn't be sure she had any left for herself right now.

He frowned, clearly not expecting this. "Forget what? Our deal?"

"Our deal! Our…whatever this is. All of it. I don't care anymore." She turned back to the door, tears making her vision blur as she reached for the doorknob, when something hard hit her back, and then slid to the ground.

She froze, momentarily stunned, and then looked at

the ground, where a snowball was crushed at her feet.

She glared at Noah. "Did you just throw a snowball at me?"

He gave a lopsided grin. One that sort of made her stomach flip. A little. "Seemed like the best way to get your attention in the moment."

"My attention? What are you, twelve?"

"I thought that was on your list. A snowball fight? Your list of Christmas traditions?" His eyes crinkled at the corner into a smile, and as much as she wanted to be mad at him, or even just plain disappointed in him, she couldn't be.

"You noticed that?"

"I notice a lot of things about you," he said, his voice so low, she almost wasn't sure that she'd heard correctly. He took a step forward, closing the distance between them. "Just so we're clear, I didn't come here because I'm mad about the decorations."

"You didn't?" Did that mean he was actually happy about them?

"I'm not going to say I'm happy about it." Well, there went that theory. He trudged across the snowy path, closer to the cottage. "But I have to give you points for trying."

She bit back a smile. That was something. And she'd take it. "So why did you come then?"

"To ask you a question. A favor, actually."

A favor? But favors were the sort of things families

called in. Or friends. And they weren't really friends, were they? She stared at him, across the snowy path, and she knew that despite everything her head was telling her, in her heart there was a soft spot for this man. And maybe even something more.

"I have to head to Boston for the night. Do you think you could keep an eye on Murphy?"

"I'd love to!" She smiled, loving the idea of snuggling with the furry guy all night. "Isn't Boston where your cousin lives?"

He shoved his hands into the pockets of his jeans. "Just for one night. I have some…business to take care of before Christmas."

She sucked in a breath, barely willing to let it out when she considered that maybe her plan was working, that maybe she had managed to thaw Scrooge's heart. But she didn't want to push her luck, not yet.

"I have a question for you too," she said, and she did, but a part of her didn't want him to go just yet.

He tipped his head, seeming to be in no rush either. "Oh, yeah?"

"Since when are you into Christmas traditions?" she asked, dropping her hand from the doorknob.

"Well," he said slowly, as he stepped up onto the porch and pointed at the roof of the awning. "You do know that's mistletoe over your head, right?" he asked, his voice low and suggestive as he looked down to meet her eye.

"Is it?" She gulped. And here she'd assumed it was just

a sprig of greenery. Something to match her wreath. She swatted him on the shoulder. "Noah Branson, are you schooling me on Christmas now?"

"I learned from the best," he said, giving her a slow smile. He leaned down, and she realized with a skip of her heart that he was actually going to kiss her. That he felt it. All the feelings, all the things she'd sensed between them these past few days.

She leaned up, her head telling her she should make an excuse, walk away, get back into the cottage and close the door, but the other part of her, the part that still dared to dream and hope, won out. It always did. Maybe that was her downfall. Or maybe, this time...

Oh. The man could certainly do more than run a cookie company. He could kiss. Soft and slow and hitting all the right places.

She sighed when he pulled away, and her cheeks felt flushed. "That was a surprise," she managed.

"I figured it was about time that I surprised you for a change," he said, stepping back into the snow.

But it wasn't the first time he'd surprised her, she thought. It might have just been the best surprise. So far.

"I'll see you when I get back?" he asked as he walked to his truck.

"I'll be here," she said as she walked back into the cottage. After all, he'd just given her a new reason to stay.

Chapter Twelve

It was dusk by the time Noah arrived back in Oyster Bay the next day, the plans in place, the details confirmed. His future suddenly wide open.

He drove slowly down Main Street, the contempt he usually held for it replaced with a strange appreciation for its charm, and a sense of loss he couldn't pinpoint. What could have been, he supposed.

He came to a stop at the last light in town, watching as an older woman ushered a small child across the street. So much could have been, and now, well.

The lights in the big house were all on as he pulled up the driveway, and instead of feeling annoyed, he was almost grateful for the rare opportunity to not come home to a dark house. It was never empty, thanks to Murphy. Last night had been the first night he'd spent without the little guy, and he missed him, felt his absence, and hated the silence of his hotel room. It left too much room for memories, for worry. For something worse, something he'd hoped to avoid by getting out of town for a night. Guilt.

Everything came with a cost. That's what Allie had told him this weekend. She was right, he knew it. But nothing felt certain anymore. What had all once felt like a clear-cut decision now felt grey and shady.

He stopped his truck at the side of the house and hopped out. His luggage could wait, and his files and paperwork would go to the office with him in the morning. A note taped to the kitchen door fluttered in the wind. "Murphy's at the cottage with me," he read aloud and smiled as he climbed back into the driver seat.

He needed to see his dog, but he wanted to see Kelly. The memory of their kiss had kept him company the entire drive to Boston, but once he was at Allie's townhouse, it was all business, and his mind had been busy, distracted since then. Now, now he wondered what it would be like to see her again, the pull of the attraction, the comfort of being heard, and maybe even understood for the first time in so long. So damn long.

The tree they had decorated filled the front window, the lights casting a warm glow in the dark forest, and for one, brief moment, it looked like a different cottage. It was small and quaint and decorated for the holidays. Some might even say it looked welcoming.

But if he closed his eyes, he could still feel the dread he had come to associate with the structure, the way his step would slow as he walked home from school, his heart gaining speed as he anticipated his mother's mood. Sometimes she'd be happy, but those bursts were short lived, and usually, usually she was just angry. Angry for the way her life had turned out. Angry that she had let a man ruin her potential. Angry that she had him, Noah had come to realize this at some point in his childhood.

Well. Soon this house would be gone.

But Kelly, he thought, thinking of what he was really implying…would she be gone, too? He pushed back the desire to kiss her again, right here and now, the moment he walked through the door. But being impulsive, not thinking things through, it hadn't gotten him anywhere. And people had paid for it. He'd paid for it.

From here on out, things would be different.

*

Murphy let out a bark and jumped off the couch where they'd been enjoying a Christmas movie for the last hour, before Kelly even noticed the headlights or heard the crunch of tires on the snow.

She held him back from the door, so he wouldn't go rushing out and get lost in the woods, but the dog wriggled under her hands, making it impossible to reach for the knob. "Come on in!" she called out, laughing.

Noah was only partway through the door when Murphy leapt at him. Noah hunched down to let him lick his face, finally saying, "Enough, buddy," when the dog showed no signs of stopping.

Kelly stepped back as Noah rose to his feet, his gaze lingering on hers for a moment. His coat was unbuttoned but his cheeks were flushed from the cold and his eyes were warm and lingering, making her stomach flutter.

"Hello there," she said, giving him a coy grin.

He matched her smile, but something in his eyes seemed to go a little flat, as if he knew something he was holding back. "Thanks for taking care of Murphy," he said.

"I hope you don't mind that he's here. But he seemed lonely last night when I took him for his walk."

"I appreciate it. You're kind to him. And to me." Noah patted the dog on the head when he nuzzled against his leg.

She shifted on her feet, waiting to see if he'd something more, if he'd continue things where they'd left off, but his eyes were shifting around the room. Around his old home. Remembering what Hannah had said about his mother, she tried to pull him back to the present.

"How did the meeting go?" Kelly asked, the hope in her voice betraying her inner most feelings. She couldn't help it, she wanted to hear him say it. He wasn't going to sell the company. No one would lose their jobs before the holidays. He was the man she believed him to be.

"Good." He sat down to pat Murphy on the head, and the dog let out a soft groan of happiness.

"He missed you when you were gone," Kelly said, coming to sit next to him on the couch. "Though I can't say that I minded having him to myself for a night."

"I won't be spending as much time away from him come Friday," Noah remarked, still scratching Murphy behind the ears.

Kelly frowned, not quite sure she followed his train of thought. "Oh? What happens on Friday?"

"The papers get signed." Noah smiled, but it didn't quite meet his eyes.

"The papers get signed?" Kelly couldn't hide her shock.

He frowned at her. "I told you about it—"

"You did." Kelly blinked, trying to digest the information which was so contrary to what she'd convinced herself of all night and day. "But then you said you were going to meet with your cousin, and I guess…" She looked up at him, but he was just frowning at her, as if she weren't making any sense. And maybe she wasn't. Maybe it was all wishful thinking. Something she'd done a lot lately.

"I have no reason to keep the company," he said bluntly.

"Yes, you do!" she insisted. "It's your grandmother's legacy. You said so yourself!"

"Wrong," he said tightly. "The cookies were her legacy. She had nothing to do with the company, and according to talk around town, she wouldn't have approved of it, either."

"But she liked sharing her cookies with people! You said that! Everyone says that! You're just going to stop all that? End it all?"

He stayed silent for a moment. His jaw twitched, and his eyes...those soft blue eyes went hard as steel. "Allie and I went over everything, and we made our final decision. There is no reason for us to continue running the company. I'm not happy, and she's eager to sell out and move onto something else. She was never invested like..."

"Like you were?"

Noah said nothing. "We're selling the company. Friday."

Christmas Eve. "So you're just going to throw it all away? Just like you're going to tear down this cottage? Your childhood home."

He frowned as he got to his feet. "I hear you've been listening to talk around town."

"Noah." She reached out to take his hand but he stood still, a wall, the same stone-faced man she had met that first day in town, not the one who had slowly taken down his walls, let her in, let her care.

"What about the people who work at the company? It's Christmas. Their jobs!"

"I told you—"

"I know." She shook her head bitterly. "It's not personal. At least, that's what you say." Only it was personal, and she wasn't sure how he couldn't see that.

Maybe it was because it just wasn't personal to him.

"I don't like to get personal," he said. "I'm not good at it."

"About work? Or about everything else?" She hadn't heeded the warnings, not from her sisters, not from herself. She'd fallen for a bad guy. Again. "About me?"

"This isn't about you, Kelly. This is about me, about something I have to do."

"Which is what, exactly? Turn your back on everything you have left? What remains of your family, your memories?" She shook her head, thinking what a sad man stood before her. "So basically you were only interested in me because you thought I'd be gone right after the first of the year?"

She stared at him, waiting for him to correct her, but instead he said nothing at all.

"I didn't stand a chance with you, did I?" She felt the tears burn the back of her eyes but she refused to let them fall.

"With the cottage? The deal?" He shook his head. His eyes were resigned. "No."

"I meant with us. This stopped being about the deal a long time ago, Noah. But then, with you, I guess it's always about business." She stared at him, anger causing her blood to rush in her ears, and for a moment, one split-second, she saw his gaze soften.

"It's not always about business, Kelly. I like you. You're the only one who got to know me. No one has done that in a long time."

She nodded. It was true, she was sure, only now, she wasn't so sure she liked what she saw. "But you knew that you weren't going to let me stay. That I couldn't convince you."

"I do not believe in all this Christmas stuff, no. Isn't there something you don't believe in?" he asked.

She thought of everything. The gifts. The dinner. The kiss. The impossible deal he'd agreed to, knowing that she would fail. He'd given her hope, but it had been false hope.

She nodded her head bitterly. "Love," she said sadly. "I don't believe in love."

He looked at her, quietly, not daring to argue, perhaps, until he finally said the words that took the last bit of hope she had and snuffed it out. "Guess that makes two of us," he said.

Kelly watched as he hooked Murphy's leash to the dog's collar and led him outside. A day ago she would have argued, would have called out, would have pointed out that he loved Murphy, and that this counted for something, and that he wasn't the Scrooge he was made out to be.

Only right now, thinking of how hard his heart was, how unwavering and cold he was in his decision to banish all memories of the grandmother who'd loved him, she couldn't be so sure that statement would be accurate anymore.

The man was going to ruin Christmas for dozens of

people who didn't see it coming.

Just like he had ruined Christmas for her.

Chapter Thirteen

The knock on the door the next evening was one of three people, Kelly estimated. Noah, Hannah, or Evie. Considering how she'd left things off with both Noah and her oldest sister, she could safely assume it was Evie. She was right.

She opened the door to see Evie standing on the front step, holding a bottle of wine and a bag of food. She grinned and said, "Dinner?"

A week ago, Kelly would have thought that nothing could beat this. A night by the Christmas tree with holiday movies and snacks, with her sister? But now her heart felt heavy, she was exhausted from finishing all the stockings by today's final order, and the realization that everything she'd hoped for this holiday had not happened.

"I suppose Hannah talked to you," she said as she uncorked the wine and filled two glasses.

Evie set the bag of food on the coffee table near the couch. "She did. She feels bad. So do I. We wanted this to be a special Christmas for you. For all of us."

Kelly shook her head. "I expected too much. And then, when Hannah said those things, it just confirmed my worst fear."

"Which is?"

Kelly hesitated as she took the seat beside her sister. Loraine was such a sensitive topic, and the last thing she wanted to do was upset her other sister, too, especially now, when they were finally forming a relationship. "I've always felt like I have two families. The one in California. And the one here." Now, she realized that Hannah no doubt felt the same. Maybe, even worse.

"We all feel that way. Even me." Evie gave a resigned smile.

"You? But…" She'd been about to say that Evie didn't have a relationship with Loraine, but maybe that didn't mean she didn't still feel torn.

Evie sat back against the couch, her wine glass untouched on the table. Now Kelly remembered that Evie rarely drank, didn't like the feel of it, and that she'd probably only poured herself a glass for the same reason that Kelly had made herself an extra cup of coffee when Hannah had come over. Because she wanted to try. She wanted to bond. She wanted what Kelly wanted. Maybe what they all did.

"When Hannah went out to California, I said some things I regret. I made her feel guilty for going, I told her that our dad, me, our cousins, Mimi, at the time our aunt and uncle, that we should all be enough. I made her feel like I didn't understand why she was going, but the truth was that I did. She wanted to know you. She wanted to know our mother. And a part of me envied her for having the courage to do it."

Kelly tried to process what her sister was saying. "You mean, you wanted to get to know me?"

Evie leaned forward and squeezed her hand. "Of course I wanted to get to know you. You were my sister. How could I not? But I felt torn. I felt too loyal to my father. I was afraid to hurt him. And with Hannah gone it was like I was all he had left."

"But Hannah said he never gave her a hard time." If anything, Chip had been completely supportive, but underneath his tough shell, Hannah had suspected he was hurt.

"He didn't. He understood. Of course he missed her, but he knows that he's not her only family. Neither am I." Evie reached forward for her wine glass, taking a minuscule sip. No doubt one glass would last all night, and probably not be finished. But Kelly liked that thought. It meant that Evie wasn't planning on leaving anytime soon.

"It's hard, trying to balance everything. Loraine doesn't even know that I'm here." Kelly considered this. Perhaps

Hannah had replied to the text. Perhaps she had revealed the secret that Kelly had been keeping from her mother—and why? Year after year Loraine did as she pleased for the holiday. Why was Kelly so afraid to tell Loraine where she was?

"Afraid she wouldn't understand?" Evie opened the bag of food and set crackers, cheese, and some dried fruits out on a paper plate that Kelly was quick to note had a beautiful holiday theme to it.

"Afraid she'd be hurt," Kelly realized. She glanced sidelong at her sister. "Is that dumb?"

"To consider your mother's feelings? No." She hesitated as she unwrapped a wedge of brie from its plastic wrap. "Sometimes I wonder if she's waiting for me to reach out to her, the way Hannah eventually did."

Kelly considered this. "Perhaps." In a way, she hoped this was true. It would mean Loraine felt bad for what she'd done, that she didn't know how to make it right. That she had a heart. Even at Christmas. "Do you think you ever will?"

"I haven't decided yet," Evie said. She broke off a piece of cheddar and set it on a cracker. "For now, my life feels full. And with you here, I no longer feel so torn. It weighed on me, knowing that you were out there, that we'd never spoken or met, and that I didn't want to let my family here down by going off in search of you. But from Hannah I realized that it's okay to have both families in my life. Maybe they won't cross over. Maybe it will be hard to balance. But it's better than choosing sides."

Kelly looked down at the paper plate Evie had handed her, wishing she could push aside this dread in her chest, enjoy the feast her sister had brought over, but all she could think about was Loraine's unanswered texts. Christmas Eve was tomorrow. Did Loraine know she wasn't coming home?

"Loraine is never going to be the person I want her to be," Kelly said. She'd heard Dr. Chandler say this to her so many times over the years, but she'd never fully admitted it to herself. Every disappointment felt fresh, and every sprig of hope was hard to pass up.

"No," Evie said sadly, "Probably not. But you have other people to fill those needs. You have Hannah, and, well, I'd like to think that you know you have me. And I hope that our mother can understand that. Maybe she will, if you give her a chance."

Kelly nodded. She had been too worried about Loraine's reaction to even admit her whereabouts, but now, omitting the truth felt worse. It felt like she was hiding something. Or, rather, someone. How would her mother react to her spending the holidays with her sisters this year? She'd never given her the chance to find out.

"I'll be honest with her," Kelly said, deciding to text when Evie went home for the night. "I feel bad about the things I said to Hannah. Is she mad at me?"

Evie shook her head. "She knows it's complicated. Besides, isn't that what sisters do? Argue and make up?"

She grinned. "You'll still join us tomorrow at the tree lighting?"

Kelly began loading up her plate as her spirits lifted. "There's no way I'm missing it." She'd only been hearing about it since she was fourteen, imagining how festive and special it would be to gather around the tree while the choirs sang carols and everyone held a single candle, before going off to their homes, where trees would light the windows and stockings would be hung from the mantles, waiting to be filled.

She eyed the small mantle now. The three stockings she'd made for her sisters had not yet been hung, but she had a better idea for them. For this year.

"You look happy," Evie observed. "Something to do with the owner of this, admittedly, adorable cottage?"

Immediately, Kelly's smile fell. "No."

"Uh-oh." Evie popped a grape in her mouth. "Didn't we warn you about him?"

"I thought he was different," Kelly sighed. She stared at her plate of cheese and crackers and fruit. Even the joy of comfort foods had escaped her, and that was saying something, considering she'd lived off junk for more than a month after Brian had left her.

She must really have it bad.

"Maybe he is different," Evie said. "Maybe we were all wrong."

Kelly looked at her for a long time, unsure if her sister was just trying to lift her spirits. "You mean that?"

"You must have seen something good in him," Evie

said. "I don't think you imagined it."

Kelly picked up a cracker and took a bite, thinking of the way Noah interacted with Murphy. There was no denying that there was love there, and a heart. It was real. As real as that kiss had been.

Or maybe she'd just gotten caught up in the magic of Christmas.

*

Noah sat in the conference room, next to Allie, and across from the Dubrow Foods team. The room was quiet, negotiations had been finalized, and all of the paperwork had been signed by Allie in Boston. Jerry Dubrow finished signing the contracts and slid the stack to Noah. All eyes shifted to him.

He pulled in a breath and picked up his pen, plucked off the cap and stared at the line. It could all be over with a simple signature.

But what would be over? The looks he got when he went into town? The accusations that he had turned a charming, local company full of heart and happiness into a national brand that was stripped of anything personal aside from the damn picture of him as a boy? Aside from the jingle?

Gran had loved making those cookies. Loved handing them out. Loved selling them in the shops in town. And he had foolishly thought she would love for more people to have those cookies. And maybe, just maybe, a small part of him thought that she would be proud of him, for making something of himself.

Only what had he made? A company he was about to hand over to someone else? Someone who had never met Gran and probably couldn't care less about the backstory of the company, other than how it might influence profits?

He'd created a company, full of hard-working people, that were all about to lose their jobs, as of five o'clock today. And tomorrow was Christmas. And no matter how bad Christmas was in the big house, Gran always tried to make it special. She never gave up hope.

Allie was looking at him now, her eyes darting in silent communication. She was waiting for him to sign the papers. They all were. He reached for his water glass, took a long sip, even though his throat felt tight, and he knew then that he'd made his decision.

He was about to let a lot of people down. But not the people sitting at their desks, planning up Valentine's Day cookies. And not the people of Oyster Bay, who once took pride in knowing that they had a part in the small, special company.

And not Gran. He wouldn't let her down. At least, he'd try not to.

He put the cap back on his pen, feeling the heat of his cousin's glare. "Noah," she all but hissed.

He turned to her, seeing the fear in her eyes. "I'm happy to buy you out if that is your wish." He knew it was nowhere near the sum Dubrow was offering, but it gave her an out, and he wasn't sure if she would take it. Eventually, he decided, she would.

"Noah." Her mouth was pinched, her skin paler than usual.

He shook his head. "I'm sorry, Allie, but I just can't do it. It's not...it's not what Gran would want." And of that, he was certain.

A plate of Keepsake's original sugar cookies were on a platter in the middle of a table, and for the first time in years, they looked so appetizing, that he couldn't resist. He reached out and took one, ignoring Allie's insistent pleas to sit down, cool off, take a moment to collect himself.

He took a bite of the cookie, feeling something in his chest lift. It was Gran's recipe. As pure and simple as if he were sitting in her sunny kitchen, a glass of milk at his side.

He loved those cookies. He'd just lost a part of himself along the way.

The Dubrow team was muttering amongst themselves now, and Jerry frowned deeply at him across the table. "What is this? What's going on?

"The company's not for sale," Noah said, closing his leather-bound folder. Allie couldn't sell without his share. She knew it. They knew it. He saw their attorney loosen his tie.

The men across the table from him gaped. "Noah. With all due respect, it's the day before Christmas—"

"And we're sitting here conducting business. You should be home, with your families, not sitting in this boardroom, discussing margins and profits." Noah shook his head. He should be with Murphy. In the big house. He should be anywhere but here. Monday, then he'd be back. But not today.

"Now, if you'll excuse me, there's something I need to do." He pushed back his chair and stood, ignoring all the slacked jaws, and gathered up his papers. His surroundings were a blur as he walked back to his office, the same route he had taken every day for the past five years, the same route he would take for five more years, and five more after that.

Only this time, it would be different. Keepsake Cookies was a local company. It was once the pride of Oyster Bay. And it was time to bring it back to the people who had supported it and believed in it. He had the infrastructure, the staff, the budget, and the plan. But he'd been missing the heart. That was what Gran had brought to each cookie.

"Meeting over so soon?" Meryl looked up from her computer screen in surprise as he passed her desk, once again, nearly knocking her small tree to the ground.

"I'm sorry," he said, setting it upright.

Meryl was already out of her chair, scrambling to gather the ornaments that had fallen before someone stepped on them. "Don't worry. I'll take care of this." She moved the tree away from the edge of the desk, right next to the picture of her daughter, in the homemade frame.

Noah paused, then said, "It's Christmas Eve." To him it had been just been another Friday, but to everyone else, it was a day to enjoy, to celebrate.

And for the first time in a long time, he had something to celebrate too.

"It is," she gave a tight smile as she scooted her chair back under the desk.

Maybe it was the sugar high from the cookie, or maybe it was just sheer relief, but Noah suddenly blurted, "Take the rest of the day off. And send out a memo alerting the staff first, if you don't mind?"

"Not at all, Mr. Branson!" Meryl's eyes were so wide, he could see the whites all around them, and she quickly pulled up a fresh email document and began pounding at the keyboard.

Noah grinned and opened his office door, stopping short when he remembered one more thing he should do. "Oh? And Meryl?"

Meryl's expression folded in disappointment as she stopped typing and swiveled her chair to face him. "Yes, sir?"

He grinned. "Merry Christmas!"

*

The big tree in the center of town square was lit all the way to the highest branch, and around its base, it seemed that the entire town had gathered, every person holding a single candle that flickered and glowed in the moonlight.

Evie and Kelly arrived together, and the first person to greet them at the opening to the square was Hannah.

"I'm sorry," was the first thing she said.

Kelly shook her head. "No, I'm sorry. I had all sorts of expectations about this Christmas, and I didn't stop to realize that it was perfect in its own way."

Well, almost perfect. There was still the disappointment about how things had gone with Noah that weighed heavily in her chest. Still, she did her best to push that aside as she and her sisters collected their candles and joined the crowd.

"Lucy's school chorus is leading the event tonight," Hannah said proudly. She craned her neck to see over the heads of those who stood in front of them, to the children who were now standing in two straight lines under the tree, all bundled up in their winter coats and hats.

Kelly had trouble deciphering which one was Lucy until she spotted the bright pink puffer coat and the smiling face that showed only a hint of nerves. A few kids shifted on their feet, others shivered in the cold, and a group of adults were huddled in conversation.

"I wonder what the delay is." Hannah looked worried when Dan approached.

"The older kids from band were supposed to accompany them, but they got delayed in a concert at Serenity Hills. I guess the crowd kept asking for an encore, and seeing as most of the old folks wouldn't be able to make it here tonight, the teacher didn't have the heart to say no."

"But what about Lucy and these kids?" Evie asked. She glanced over at Liam who was jogging over to them. "Don't worry. You're not late. There's a delay."

Dan shrugged. "Looks like they'll have to go it alone. I just hope they can stay on tune."

"Doesn't anyone play guitar or something? Flynn can open the music shop and let someone borrow an instrument," Liam suggested.

"Good idea. I'll ask around." Dan handed Hannah his candle and walked over to the nearest group of people.

Kelly watched him go, wandering from person to person. She knew someone who played the guitar, but she kept her mouth quiet. Noah insisted he didn't play, not anymore. Besides, he wouldn't be here anyway.

Hannah let out a heavy sigh. "I feel bad for Lucy. She was nervous as it was to perform for the whole town like this."

"Kids bounce back," Evie assured her, but it did little to take the disappointment out of Hannah's face.

She'd make a good mom someday, Kelly thought. She knew Hannah had reservations about getting involved with Dan, being a stepmother, when she'd had no mother figure herself for most of her life, but it came naturally. Or maybe it came from her other family. From Chip.

Suddenly there was a round of applause and Dan came jogging up to them, out of breath, steam escaping his mouth as he explained. "It's all settled. I think you're in for a surprise."

Kelly wasn't sure she was up for any more surprises. As it was, she nearly jumped every time she heard someone's phone ring. She'd texted Loraine about her decision not to come home this Christmas, and she was yet to receive a response. Hoping for a distraction, she clutched her candle and leaned to the side, trying to get a better view of Lucy and her friends as the music started and the children began singing a classic holiday song. The guitarist was a natural, playing just loud enough to lead the group but not too loud to overshadow their small voices, and Kelly smiled as she took in the sounds that filled the otherwise silent town square. It was a beautiful night. Not too cold. Small flakes of snow were just starting to fall. It was perfect, really. Or it would have been, if—

Wait. She blinked, not quite sure if her imagination had truly gotten the better of her, but no, it was real. It was Noah. With a guitar. Leading the children in their song.

Evie elbowed her and jutted her chin to the tree. "You really were right about him."

Was she? Kelly wanted so badly to believe that was true, that Noah wasn't the Scrooge everyone thought he was, that he really had a heart, but she just couldn't quite shake the thought of what he'd done today, how many people had gone home for their Christmas holiday with fear instead of hope, with worry instead of happiness.

From across the crowd, he caught her eye. She froze, unsure what to do. She waited to see if he would smile, but his gaze was intense, and lingering, until a change in song made him shift his attention.

Kelly felt like she didn't breathe again until the children's chorus was finished, and Noah unstrapped the guitar from his shoulder and handed it back to a man who packed it up in its case.

She looked around, to see if he would approach her, but the crowd was thick, and everyone was cheering as the lights came up on the tree, illuminating the entire night sky, for one, truly magical moment.

Kelly turned as the crowd grew loud, muttering their Christmas wishes, shaking hands, some people hugging, as they all headed back toward Main Street. Hannah had disappeared to find Dan and Lucy and Evie had wandered over to where the Harper cousins were gathered. Kelly stood near the entrance to the square, waiting for her sisters, watching as faces she didn't recognize, and some that she did, walked past her, many people stopping to nod, to smile, to wish her a happy holiday.

There was a tap on her shoulder, one that made her stomach drop and her heart begin to race, and she turned, even though she didn't want to turn, because she didn't think she wanted to hear what he had to say, only to find that it wasn't Noah at all. It was a child, one that she recognized from Lucy's chorus, holding a basket of...cookies.

Keepsake cookies, she realized.

"Christmas cookie?" the child asked, handing her an individually wrapped cookie in the shape of a bell.

Kelly's throat felt tight as she accepted the gift and looked around to see other children doing exactly the same, even Lucy, in her bright pink coat, happily handing out cookies to each person as they left the event.

Just as Sandra Branson used to do, a long, long time ago.

"They're good," a voice behind her said. A deep voice. A voice she hadn't dared to think about and had thought she'd never hear again.

She turned to look up at him, standing there, with his hands in his pockets, a hesitant smile on his mouth. "Really. I ate six of them on the way home from the office."

"I thought you hated cookies," she said, feeling stiff and uncertain of where this conversation was going and what he was doing here.

"I hated myself," he said, managing to surprise her all over again. He pulled in a breath, sizing her up. "You were right. I was a Scrooge. I had no heart. And I didn't believe in love. Somewhere along the way, I got lost. I blamed this town for what they did to my mother, then I blamed them again for what they did to me. I never stopped to think about my part in it."

She held her breath, wanting to ask, but afraid of the answer. How much could people really change?

"I've decided not to sell the company," he said, and she couldn't be sure the shock didn't show in her face.

She swallowed hard, still barely able to believe it. "What made you change your mind?"

"You," he said. "This town. You brought me back into it. You reminded me of the happy memories I had. With Gran. Even in that cottage. You made me believe."

Kelly blinked hard. It was just a saying, not a promise. Not…

"The cottage is yours, Kelly. You deserve it. Not because of our deal, but because you love it, because you see the good in it."

Tears stung the back of her eyes, and the cold wind wasn't helping matters. "I saw the good in you, too."

He pulled in a breath as he stepped toward her, and she wanted to pull away, to not let him get close. To not let another person let her down. But his hand was warm on hers, and his eyes, those eyes, the same kind eyes as the little boy on the tag of that Christmas tin.

"I hope you still see the good in me," he said. "I was hoping, if you do decide to stay in the cottage, that, well, maybe we could start again?"

Stay in the cottage. Stay in Oyster Bay. She hadn't really thought it was possible, but so many things suddenly were.

"I'd like that," she said, giving him a slow smile.

"You coming, Kelly?" Hannah called out to her.

Kelly squeezed Noah's hand. "I'll be right back." She walked over to her sister and did something that surprised her, more than anything else had surprised her this

Christmas. "You go ahead. These are your traditions." She glanced back and Noah and gave her sister a knowing smile. "And I'm ready to start some of my own."

"I'll see you tomorrow then," Hannah said, giving her a pat on the arm as she walked off with Dan and Lucy, the three of them joining hands. Kelly watched them go for a moment. A happy family. A beautiful sight.

Tomorrow, Kelly thought, leaning back to take in the full height of the sparkling tree. Christmas. In Oyster Bay. She'd actually gone and done it, she realized, as she walked back to Noah, who was waiting for her at the sidewalk. Only this Christmas hadn't turned out to be anything like she'd planned.

It had been better.

Epilogue

Christmas Day had finally arrived, but rather than springing to life, Main Street was quiet, still, and perfectly calm.

Kelly took a moment to soak it all in, from the garland that was wrapped around every lamppost, to the twinkle lights that framed each storefront window. Beside her, she heard Noah give a sigh of exasperation, and she finally slid him a smile. He had stopped the car for a full five minutes by now, after all.

"Can we go now?" he asked, but she could tell by the gleam in his eyes that he would have stayed there for another five minutes, parked at the edge of town, if she'd asked him.

"Yes," she said, as her stomach rolled over. This was

it. The moment she had been fearing, the day she was going to meet Chip Donovan. And even though her sisters had reassured her that their father would welcome her with open arms, she still felt anxious. "I just need to make a call first."

"I need to fill up on gas anyway," he said, even though Kelly noticed the truck still had half a tank left in it. He knew. She was calling Loraine. She was confronting her past. Her present. And daring to plan for the future.

They pulled into a station at the edge of town, and Noah pushed open the door, pulling his wallet out of his back pocket. Kelly took a deep breath and brought up her mother's cell number, and, with a push of her thumb, connected the call. It rang twice before Loraine's voice came on, breathless, and, as usual, distracted.

"Did I catch you at a bad time?" It was always a bad time, but the disappointment still hung in her chest.

"I was just putting the turkey in the oven!" Loraine surprised her by saying.

So she'd actually done it. Cooked a dinner. Done the whole holiday thing. For a moment she felt that tug in her chest again, wondering if she'd made the right choice, but this year, this was where she wanted to be.

She glanced out the window at Noah, who gave her a thumbs-up of encouragement through the window.

Strike that. Make that, this was where she was meant to be.

"It sounds really nice," she said, and it did. It sounded lovely.

"It gave your father and me a chance to bond," Loraine said. "Are you enjoying your ski trip?"

So Hannah hadn't ratted her out then, hadn't gotten involved, had kept her relationship with each member of the family of her own, and allowed Kelly to do the same. She should have trusted that would be the case.

"I'm actually not at the lodge. I'm in…" *Just say it. Say it.* "I'm with my sisters this Christmas, and I hope that you can understand that."

There was a moment of silence, and Kelly didn't even realize she was holding her breath until Loraine said, "That sounds like a very nice way to spend Christmas."

Kelly gulped. It *was* a nice way to spend Christmas. "I'm thinking of staying here, in Oyster Bay, for a while. I got a job, a gig really, selling my knitwear. But maybe, when I come back to pack up my apartment, you could help me?"

It was the first time in years that she had dared to ask her mother directly for anything, for fear of rejection, for fear of the inevitable disappointment that had tended to follow. She knew Dr. Chandler wouldn't approve. He would ask why she couldn't accept things as they were, limitations and all, why she held out hope.

Because it's Christmas, Kelly thought. And Christmas was a time to believe.

"I'd like that," Loraine said. "I'd like that a lot."

Kelly smiled and ended the call as Noah climbed back into the truck. "All good?" He looked at her warily, and she loved that he cared, that he got it, that he didn't press for more.

"Better than good," she said.

They arrived at the inn in what felt like seconds, considering there was no traffic and the Harper House was just on the edge of town. The house looked just as welcoming and festive as it had the first time she'd come here, but her tread was slower as they walked along the salt-sprinkled path, and even as they pushed through the door, to the sounds of carols being played on the piano and people chatting and laughing, Kelly's heart was racing with nerves.

"Here, let me take that coat from you," a man said as he helped her slide it off her shoulders. "Ah, my niece has a coat just like this." He grinned as he hooked it on a hanger, but then did a double-take as he turned back to her.

Kelly's pulse was pounding in her ears. The room around her went still and quiet.

It was Chip. She would know it in a moment. Know it from the warmth in his kind blue eyes, from the smile that crinkled their corners. This was the man who had raised her sisters. Her family.

"Kelly." His voice was low and husky and without saying another word, he leaned in and hugged her, holding her close, dismissing every mile that had been placed between them, every memory she had missed, every event she had longed to be a part of. Every fear she'd had of being blamed, shunned, rejected.

She was part of it now. In the fold. Family.

"This is Noah," she said, pulling away, noticing the tears that misted Chip's eyes.

He cleared his throat, straightened his shoulders, and held out a hand. "I hear you're back in local business."

Noah scratched the back of his head. "Word travels fast in this town." After all, it was just this morning that Liam published a front-page article about Keepsake Cookies' plan to bring the company back to Oyster Bay in the New Year, with a focus on supporting local shops and restaurants.

And sometimes, Kelly thought, that was a good thing.

"I'd love to work something onto the menu at The Lantern," Chip said, and Noah's face lit into a smile.

Kelly glanced across the room, at the sisters dressed in red and green, and only then did she remember the stockings that she still had for them. One for each of them, meant to be their gifts today. Only looking around the room, she suddenly realized that by coming here she'd found more than just her sisters. She'd found family. And community. And maybe even love.

The stockings didn't stop at three. And she was so grateful for that.

*

It wasn't until the turkey had been carved and the pies had been eaten that Noah leaned in and whispered to her, "I haven't given you your gift yet."

She looked at him in surprise, and then, horror. "But I...I didn't give you a gift."

"Are you kidding me?" He looked at her like she was crazy. "You gave me a Christmas tree. Cookies. And so much more."

"Well," she said, fighting off a smile, "I won't take full responsibility..."

He laughed. "Yes, you will. And I have a feeling a year from now you'll be throwing it in my face over something too."

A year from now. Where would she be? Here in this inn, with Noah at her side and her sisters across the table? A year ago, she had been longing to know Evie, and today hadn't even felt like a dream worth having.

"Here," he slid her a small box, unwrapped, with a bow taped to the top. Clearly, he was not used to this sort of thing, and that made this oh so much more special.

She glanced around the table, but everyone was busy talking, Lucy and Emma were running off to play, and Mimi was adjusting Earl's bow tie, even though he was already starting to nod off.

Kelly opened the small box, revealing a silver bracelet full of charms. One was a stocking. Another was a dog. There was a tree. And a cookie. And a house.

"I wanted to give you everything on your list. Sledding on Shell Hill. Caroling door to door."

Caroling door to door! Yes, that had been on her list. Now, she couldn't help but laugh. "You really want to go caroling door to door?"

"Well, no, but you wanted to. Those were the traditions you wanted to have."

"And this?" She held up the bracelet, then set it on her wrist.

"These are the traditions we made. This Christmas."

Oh. Kelly slid the bracelet around her wrist, noticing the space for more charms. More traditions. "It's perfect."

"So you're not disappointed you didn't get to do everything on your list?"

No, she thought. She wasn't focused on the Christmases of past anymore, or on what she'd thought she'd lost. She was focused on today. On tomorrow.

She reached down to take his hand and smiled into his kind, blue eyes. "I have everything I ever wanted right here."

USA TODAY bestselling author OLIVIA MILES writes feel-good women's fiction and heartwarming contemporary romance best known for her quirky side characters and charming small town settings. She lives just outside Chicago with her husband, young daughter, and two ridiculously pampered pups.

Visit her website at www.OliviaMilesBooks.com to learn more.

Made in the USA
San Bernardino, CA
24 November 2018